AETHERIA: LOST HORIZON

ROHIT R

Made with ♥ on the Notion Press Platform
www.notionpress.com

To my father,

You've always been the compass guiding me through life's uncharted territories. Just as Ethan Turner embarks on his journey in "Lost Horizon," you've shown me that with courage and determination, we can navigate even the most treacherous paths.

Your unwavering support and belief in me have been my greatest source of strength. Through the challenges and triumphs, your wisdom has been my guiding light.

This book is a tribute to your love, your resilience, and the lessons you've imparted. Like Ethan, I hope to inspire others to face the unknown with bravery and hope.

Contents

Foreword

In the pages that follow, you will embark on a journey into the world of "AETHERIA," a realm born from imagination, nurtured by creativity, and brought to life through words. This series, beginning with "Lost Horizon," is a testament to the power of storytelling, a journey through a landscape where the boundaries of reality and fiction blur.

As the author of this series, I invite you to dive headfirst into this post-apocalyptic world, where hope persists in the face of despair, and resilience shines through the darkest of days. The characters you will meet are not merely ink on paper; they are reflections of our shared human experience, navigating a world forever altered by catastrophe.

Through these stories, I hope to remind you of the enduring strength of the human spirit, the bonds that unite us in times of adversity, and the possibility of transformation, even in the most challenging circumstances. "AETHERIA" is an exploration of courage, love, and the relentless pursuit of a better world.

So, as you turn the page and step into this world, may you find solace, inspiration, and a renewed sense of wonder. May you be reminded that, like the characters within these pages, we too have the power to shape our destinies, rewrite our stories, and dream of brighter horizons.

Preface

In the vast expanse of time, there are moments when our imaginations take flight, when we dare to envision worlds beyond our own, and when storytelling becomes a bridge between reality and dreams. "AETHERIA" is born from one such moment, a tapestry woven with threads of hope, resilience, and the enduring human spirit.

This series, commencing with "Lost Horizon," invites you to explore a world that, while steeped in fiction, echoes with the heartbeat of our shared existence. It is a world that, like our own, has been touched by catastrophe and chaos, yet refuses to surrender to despair.

In these pages, you will meet characters who, in their pursuit of truth and survival, mirror our own aspirations and struggles. They are flawed and courageous, driven by love, loss, and the profound desire for a better future. Their journey through the ruins of a once-thriving world serves as a mirror to our own collective journey.

As you immerse yourself in "AETHERIA," may you find a reflection of your own hopes and dreams, your own battles and victories. May you be inspired to confront the challenges of your world with the same determination that fuels the characters within these stories.

So, embark on this odyssey with an open heart and an adventurous spirit, for within these pages, you will discover not only a tale of survival but a celebration of the resilience that defines us all.

Acknowledgements

Writing a book is a solitary endeavor, yet its realization into a tangible work is a collaborative effort that touches the lives of many. I wish to express my deepest gratitude to all those who contributed to the creation of "Lost Horizon" and the entire "AETHERIA" series.

First and foremost, to my family and friends, for their unwavering support, encouragement, and belief in this literary journey. Your love and understanding during the late nights and countless revisions have been my pillars of strength.

To my readers, for embracing the world of "AETHERIA" and embarking on this adventure with me. Your enthusiasm and feedback have been a constant source of inspiration.

To my literary agent and publisher, for believing in the story and its potential. Your guidance and expertise have been invaluable in bringing this work to fruition.

To the talented artists and designers who contributed their skills to the book covers and merchandise, your creativity has given life to the visual aspects of "AETHERIA."

To my mentors and fellow writers, for sharing your wisdom and fostering my growth as a storyteller. Your insights have shaped the narrative in profound ways.

To the entire editorial and production team, whose dedication and hard work have transformed the manuscript into a polished book.

And finally, to the characters of "AETHERIA" themselves, for coming to life in my imagination and allowing me to share their stories with the world. They are the heart and soul of this series.

This book is a culmination of collective efforts, and I extend my deepest appreciation to all who have played a part, however big or small, in its creation.

Prologue

In the remnants of a world once vibrant and alive, a story unfolds. It is a tale of resilience, courage, and the unyielding human spirit—a story set against the backdrop of a world forever changed.

As we step into the world of "AETHERIA," we are invited to witness the echoes of a past civilization, to traverse landscapes scarred by catastrophe, and to embark on a journey of discovery and redemption.

In these pages, you will encounter characters who navigate the darkness with the flicker of hope as their guide. Their voices echo the collective longing for a better tomorrow, for a world where dreams can flourish once more.

Yet, beyond the challenges that confront them, a glimmer of possibility shines. It is a possibility that, like a spark in the night, refuses to be extinguished. It beckons us all to imagine a future where, despite the odds, humanity prevails.

So, as we delve into the heart of "AETHERIA," let us remember that even in the face of adversity, stories are born, journeys are embarked upon, and the human spirit soars.

CHAPTER ONE

Wasteland

Ethan Turner had known nothing but desolation for as long as he could remember. The world he once knew had crumbled into ruins, leaving behind a barren wasteland. Dilapidated buildings stood as solemn reminders of a time when life flourished, now reduced to decaying skeletons of a forgotten era. Nature had reclaimed what was once hers, with weeds pushing through cracks in the asphalt and vines entangling the remnants of human existence. The air hung heavy with an eerie silence, broken only by the distant howling of the wind. It whispered through the hollow spaces between crumbling walls, carrying the echoes of a bygone civilization. Amidst this desolation, Ethan, a resilient teenager, traversed the wasteland with a purpose. His determination burned brightly within him, driving him forward through the harsh realities of survival. Ethan had learned to adapt, honing his skills to scavenge for supplies that would ensure his continued existence. Every day was a battle for sustenance, for the most necessities of life. He roamed the empty streets, his footsteps echoing against the hollow silence, a solitary figure against the backdrop of desolation. His worn-out boots kicked up clouds of dust with each step, leaving traces of his solitary journey behind. The relentless sun beat down upon him, its scorching rays casting long shadows amidst the crumbling buildings. Sweat dripped down his brow, a testament to the unforgiving conditions that plagued the wasteland. It had been weeks since he encountered any signs of life or encountered valuable supplies. The wasteland seemed to stretch on endlessly, devoid of any glimmer of hope. Yet, he pressed on, his resilience unyielding.

As he pushed forward, his mind began to wander. The weight of loneliness settled heavily upon him, threatening to consume his spirit. In this desolate world, he longed for a momentary escape, a respite from the constant struggle. Seeking solace, he decided to venture into an area of the ruins he had never explored before, a part of the city that appeared strangely untouched by the chaos and destruction. Intrigue mingled with caution as he cautiously stepped into this uncharted territory. The silence here was different, almost eerie in its purity. The buildings stood tall and untouched, their walls still holding hints of their former glory. Ethan couldn't help but wonder what secrets lay hidden within these pristine structures. Could there be remnants of a forgotten civilization preserved in time? His footsteps echoed as he delved deeper into the untouched enclave. The air seemed to hold its breath as if aware of his presence. Ethan's eyes scanned his surroundings, searching for any sign of life or clues that would unravel the mystery of this forgotten corner. It was a delicate dance, balancing curiosity with the ever-present danger that lurked in every corner of the wasteland. Time seemed to stand still as he explored further, each step bringing him closer to the heart of this untouched sanctuary. The anticipation coursed through his veins, mingling with a spark of hope that had long been extinguished. For a brief moment, he dared to imagine a world where desolation could be transformed into renewal, where a flicker of life could emerge from the ashes. The desolate wasteland would always be his reality, but within its depths, Ethan held on to the belief that even the smallest discovery could ignite a glimmer of hope. With each passing moment, he embraced the uncertainty, ready to uncover the secrets that lay hidden in the untouched part of the city, a place where possibilities awaited and where the essence of survival intertwined with the resilience of the human spirit.

Curiosity propelled him forward, guiding his footsteps through the debris-strewn streets. The air was heavy, with a silence broken only by the occasional creaking of abandoned structures. The eerie stillness made his heart race, but he pressed on, determined to discover anything that could breathe life into his monotonous existence. Ethan's eyes widened at the sight before him as he turned a corner. A row of dilapidated houses stood, relatively intact compared to the rest of the cityscape. Vines and weeds crept up their decaying walls as if nature had claimed them for its own. The silence was interrupted by the distant chirping of birds, creating a surreal contrast to the desolation that surrounded him. Intrigued, Ethan cautiously stepped towards the nearest house. Its door was partially ajar, inviting him to explore further. With a mix of apprehension and curiosity, he pushed the door open, revealing a dimly lit interior filled with dust-covered furniture and forgotten memories. His eyes scanned the room, searching for any sign of useful supplies. That's when his gaze fell upon a small table, upon which lay the weathered journal. It seemed out of place amidst the abandoned furniture, its leather cover bearing the scars of time. The sight of it piqued Ethan's curiosity, and he gingerly picked it up, feeling its weight in his hands. The journal exuded an air of mystery as if it held secrets waiting to be unraveled. Ethan carefully pried it open without hesitation, his fingers trembling with anticipation. The journal seemed out of place amidst the desolation, its cover bearing the scars of a thousand forgotten stories. Ethan's heart quickened as he opened the journal, revealing yellowed pages filled with faded ink. As he perused the writings, he realized they were penned by his long-lost father, a man he had believed to be dead for years. Each word carried the weight of untold sorrow and longing. It was a bittersweet reunion with a past he had almost given up hope of ever finding.

The journal entries painted a vivid picture of a life that once was, a world teeming with vibrancy and hope. Ethan's father described the bustling streets, the laughter of children playing in the parks, and the warmth of the community. The stark contrast between the desolation that surrounded Ethan and the vibrant world described in his father's words was overwhelming. But it wasn't just the presence of his father's words that stirred Ethan's emotions; it was the message concealed within them. In the journal, his father chronicled the beauty of the world they had lost and the resilience of the human spirit. He wrote about the struggles they faced, the hardships that tested their resolve, and the unwavering determination to rebuild after every setback. These writings revealed to Ethan the strength and courage that his father possessed, even in the face of unimaginable adversity.

As he continued reading, Ethan immersed himself in a tapestry of memories, experiencing the past through his father's eyes. He felt a profound connection to the man he had never truly known, understanding the sacrifices made and the dreams that were never realized. The journal was a window into his father's soul, a testament to the love he had for his family and his unyielding hope for a better future. Tears welled up in Ethan's eyes as he realized that despite the bleakness of the present, the journal carried a message of hope.

The Message was "My Dearest Ethan,

If you're reading this, it means you've embarked on a journey of discovery, a journey that holds the key to a world of New beginnings. The road ahead might be treacherous, but your resourcefulness and determination will guide you. Remember, the answers you seek are hidden within the pages of time, waiting to be deciphered.

Look to the heavens, where stars light up the canvas of the night. The constellations hold secrets, forming a map that points to what lies beyond. Follow the path they illuminate, a celestial breadcrumb trail.

In the heart of the city, Within the echoes of forgotten chambers, you'll find symbols etched into the walls. These symbols are the threads that weave the tapestry of history. Follow their path, and let their patterns guide you.

As dawn breaks and the sun bathes the world in its golden Embrace, seek the solace of nature. The rivers that flow and the trees that stand tall—they hold whispers of truth. Listen to the melodies of the wind, for they carry stories untold.

Amongst the bustling streets, where life thrives Despite the shadows, you'll find the answers you seek in the mundane. Every day holds magic, and within the hustle and bustle, a revelation awaits.

Let your heart be your compass, Ethan. The journey you're on is more than a physical one—it's a journey of understanding, of connection. Pieces of a puzzle await your touch, waiting to be fitted together into a tapestry that reveals a new world—a world of promise.

Trust in your instincts, and let the dance of sereNdipity guide your steps. You'll uncover truths that others overlook, for your perception is a gift.

May your path be illuminated, and may your journey lead you to the horizon of a brighter future. Know that wherever you go, my love is with you, urging you forward.

With unwavering belief,

Thomas Turner"

As Ethan carefully reads his father's journal, he's drawn to the way certain letters are capitalized seemingly without a pattern. These capital letters stand out, forming an unintended sequence. Puzzled by this irregularity, Ethan begins to write down each capitalized letter as he encounters them in the text. As he does so, a pattern starts to emerge.

The letters he's gathered spell out: "N-E-W-E-D-E-N." At first, this sequence appears random, but as he studies it further, a realization dawns upon him. The letters seem to be scattered throughout the journal, forming an unintentional yet coherent pattern. "New Eden" emerges from otherwise unrelated words and sentences.

Ethan's heart quickens as he stares at the sequence. It's as if his father had left a hidden trail, guiding him toward

a discovery. He traces the letters with his finger, a mix of excitement and curiosity swirling within him. Could this be a clue his father left behind? Could "New Eden" hold the answers he's been searching for?

The realization that his father's journal itself spells out the name of the utopian city he's been seeking leaves Ethan with a sense of awe. It's a testament to his father's ingenuity, a subtle hint meant to be deciphered by someone who knows where to look. As he gazes at the letters, his determination is renewed. Armed with this newfound insight, he's more certain than ever that the path to "New Eden" lies ahead, waiting for him to uncover its secrets.

Rumors of this place had circulated among the survivors; a utopia said to be the last flicker of hope in a world consumed by darkness. It was believed that New Eden held the key to rebuilding a shattered civilization, a place where humanity could find solace and redemption. As Ethan delved deeper into the journal, he discovered that his father had been part of a secret group dedicated to protecting the knowledge of New Eden. They were called the Founders, entrusted with the responsibility of preserving the hope that lay within the sanctuary. The journal entries hinted at the existence of a map, a map that would guide the chosen ones to New Eden's hidden location. Ethan's hands trembled as he absorbed the weight of his father's revelation. A spark ignited within him, a newfound determination to uncover the truth and embark on a perilous journey to find this sanctuary. The prospect of reuniting with his long-lost family fueled his resolve. But as Ethan read on, he realized that the path to New Eden would not be easy. The world outside was filled with dangers and treachery. The remnants of humanity had turned on each other, battling for scarce resources and power. Gangs roamed the wasteland, preying on the weak and defenseless. And there were whispers of a tyrant who sought to control New Eden and exploit its potential for his gain.

CHAPTER TWO

Hidden Message

As Ethan continued to decipher his father's hidden message, the pieces of the puzzle began to fall into place. The encrypted words unveiled a tantalizing glimpse into the world of New Eden, and Ethan's curiosity grew with each revelation. The message spoke of a sanctuary, a haven untouched by the desolation of the outside world. It described a lush paradise hidden away, sheltered from the chaos and destruction that had consumed the Earth. Ethan's heart swelled with a mixture of hope and trepidation, envisioning a place where humanity could find solace and rebuild. Among the cryptic clues, the message hinted at the existence of a guiding star—a celestial beacon that would lead the way to New Eden. It spoke of an ancient legend, passed down through generations, of a radiant star that shone brighter than any other in the night sky. This star, it seemed, held the key to unlocking the path to the fabled utopia. As Ethan meticulously pieced together the clues, he discovered references to a group of resistance fighters known as the Guardians. The message spoke of their unwavering commitment to protect and preserve New Eden, to defend it from those who would exploit its abundance and purity. Ethan sensed that these Guardians would play a vital role in his journey, offering guidance and protection along the way. The message also hinted at the existence of a hidden gate—an entrance to New Eden concealed within the remnants of an ancient structure. It described a place where nature and technology converged, where the secrets of the utopia were safeguarded. Ethan envisioned a thrilling adventure through forgotten ruins and dangerous territories, all in pursuit of the gateway to a brighter future.

Sarah Turner is Ethan's younger sister, a bright and compassionate teenage girl. Despite the harshness of their world, she maintains a resilient spirit and a genuine desire to help others. Sarah possesses a natural curiosity and a thirst for knowledge, always eager to explore and learn about their decaying city. Growing up in the post-apocalyptic landscape, Sarah became an invaluable asset to their small community. She developed a talent for scavenging and resourcefulness, often discovering hidden caches of supplies and finding creative solutions to problems. Her compassionate nature led her to assist those in need, offering a helping hand to fellow survivors and providing comfort in times of hardship. Sarah's deep bond with Ethan forms the foundation of their relationship. They share a profound connection, relying on each other for support and finding solace in their shared experiences. Despite the challenges they face, Sarah's optimism and unwavering belief in a brighter future serve as a guiding light for both herself and her brother. As the world around them deteriorates, Sarah becomes increasingly concerned about the future of humanity. She yearns for a place where people can find safety, hope, and the chance to rebuild. This longing fuels her curiosity and motivates her to search for answers and potential solutions to the struggles they face.

As the sun rose on the morning of their departure, casting a golden hue over the desolation, Ethan and Sarah stood side by side, their faces etched with determination and hope. The cool breeze carried fragments of memories and whispered tales of a forgotten era as if the very air mourned the loss of what once was. The siblings observed the jagged remnants of once majestic skyscrapers, their crumbling facades testaments to the fragility of human achievements. They couldn't help but feel a pang of sadness for the city they had called home, now reduced to a labyrinth of broken dreams. Yet, amidst the ruins, they clung to a shared dream—the promise of New Eden. Their backpacks, worn and weathered, symbolized their resilience and preparedness for the unknown. Each item held a story—a canteen filled with precious water, a frayed map marked with their planned route, and a handful of scavenged rations, reminders of the struggles they had endured to survive. With their gazes fixed on the horizon, Ethan and Sarah felt the weight of the world on their shoulders. It was a world where hope had become a scarce commodity, and trust was a luxury that few could afford. But the whispers of New Eden beckoned a distant melody that refused to fade.

As they took their first steps, the cracked pavement and overgrown weeds seemed to mirror their determination to leave behind the decaying remnants of their past. The path ahead was treacherous, littered with obstacles that challenged their every move. Broken beams jutted out like skeletal fingers, a stark reminder of the fragility of their surroundings. Ethan and Sarah approached this daunting landscape with cautious steps, their senses heightened and alert. They relied on their survival instincts, honed through countless encounters with the perils of the wasteland. Each obstacle was a test. Their hands interlaced, they maneuvered through the labyrinth of fallen structures and dilapidated walls. The crumbling walls whispered stories of forgotten triumphs and shattered ambitions, their peeling paint revealing layers of lives that once flourished. Dust clung to their clothes, leaving a trail of their journey in its wake. The air tasted heavy with decay, yet, amid the desolation, they found solace in their shared purpose. Their silent communication conveyed through touches and glances, spoke volumes of their unbreakable bond, their unity becoming a beacon of hope in a desolate landscape.

Ethan and Sarah journeyed deeper into the desolation. The scorching sun beat down relentlessly, its rays searing their exposed skin. They draped a tattered cloth over their heads, shielding themselves from the relentless heat. Their water bottles were precious commodities. They rationed their meager supplies, sharing what little food and water they had, ensuring that both could sustain their energy. Their thirst and hunger gnawed at them, but their love and determination fortified their spirits. They knew that reaching New Eden meant enduring these hardships, and their shared vision of a better future kept them pushing forward.

Facing the harsh world beyond New Eden's walls, Ethan and Sarah found themselves thrust into a dangerous dance with ruthless scavengers. These scavengers, weathered by the unforgiving landscape, regarded any intruders as threats to their survival. Tensions hung in the air like a charged storm, ready to erupt at any moment.

One day, as the sun cast long shadows across the barren terrain, Ethan and Sarah stumbled upon the scavengers' makeshift camp. A wary exchange of glances followed, the scavengers eyeing them with suspicion.

Scavenger Leader: "Who're you two, wanderin' into our territory?"

Ethan, his voice steady, raised his hands in a gesture of non-hostility.

Ethan: "Just travelers, looking for a safe passage. We don't mean any harm."

Sarah, her eyes sharp, chimed in.

Sarah: "We're not here to steal or cause trouble. We understand survival."

Scavenger Leader: (gruffly) "Survival ain't about understandin'. It's about fightin' for every scrap."

Ethan: "We get it. We've faced our share of struggles out there."

Their words seemed to strike a chord, the tense atmosphere slightly easing.

Scavenger Leader: "Well, you'll need more than words to earn our trust."

Ethan's eyes met Sarah's, and they exchanged a knowing look.

Sarah: "What can we do to prove ourselves?"

The scavenger leader hesitated before finally speaking.

Scavenger Leader: "We've got a problem. A rival gang's been takin' our supplies. We could use some help gettin' 'em back."

Ethan: "If we help you, will you consider a truce?"

Scavenger Leader: "We'll consider it."

The negotiation had begun—a chance for understanding amidst the tension. Working together, they planned their approach to retrieve the stolen supplies. Under the moon's silvery gaze, they set out on their mission, each step guided by the tentative bonds of a shared goal.

As they confronted the rival gang, words turned to action. The clash was fierce, the sound of fists meeting and shouts of determination filling the night air.

Sarah: (mid-battle) "Ethan, watch your left!"

Ethan ducked, narrowly avoiding a swing. Gratitude flashed in his eyes as he acknowledged her alert.

Ethan: "Thanks!"

Their movements were a synchronized dance, born from the unspoken trust they'd cultivated. The fight was hard-won, bruises and scrapes serving as a testament to their resolve. By dawn's light, they stood victorious, the rival gang defeated.

Scavenger Leader: "You helped us, so we'll honor our end. Truce it is—for now."

Ethan extended a hand, sealing their unsteady alliance.

Ethan: "Agreed."

As they made their way back, weary but accomplished, Ethan and Sarah exchanged exhausted smiles. Through challenges and conflicts, a bridge had been built. The scavengers now saw them not only as outsiders but as allies who understood the harsh realities of their world.

As they traversed the treacherous terrain, their bodies weary and worn, Ethan and Sarah became each other's pillars of strength. They supported one another through blistered feet and aching muscles, taking turns to carry the weight of exhaustion. Each step was a testament to their unwavering commitment to one another, their love an anchor in a world that seemed determined to tear them apart. The journey was arduous, the challenges relentless, but their determination remained unyielding. Together, they pushed through the hardships, their unwavering love and unbreakable bond propelling them forward even when their bodies begged them to stop. The torrential downpour unleashed its fury upon them, a relentless assault from the heavens.

Raindrops fell like silver needles, transforming the wasteland into a waterlogged nightmare. Mud clung to their boots, weighing them down with each step. They squelched through the muck, their feet sinking deep into the earth's embrace. But Ethan and Sarah pressed on, their hands tightly clasped, pulling each other forward through the quagmire. Their determination formed an invisible shield against the biting cold, and their unwavering commitment to one another kept them moving, even as the elements threatened to freeze their resolve. With every challenge they overcame, Ethan and Sarah grew stronger. Their love and determination became the bedrock upon which they built their resilience. As they ventured closer to their destination, the thought of New Eden fueled their spirits. They had weathered the trials of the wasteland together, their bond tested and proven unbreakable. And with their shared hope guiding them, they knew that no matter what awaited them in the city of New Eden, they would face it together, hand in hand, ready to shape their destiny.

CHAPTER THREE

The Disappearance

As they ventured closer to their destination, the thought of New Eden fueled their spirits. However, as the fog of exhaustion settled upon them and their vision blurred with fatigue, Sarah suddenly stumbled. Ethan's heart clenched with panic as he reached out to steady her. But when the mist cleared, Sarah was no longer by his side. She had vanished, swallowed by the wasteland's unforgiving embrace. Ethan's world shattered in that moment, his cry of anguish echoing through the desolate landscape. He called out her name, "Sarah...Sarah...Sarah", his voice a desperate plea in the silence. But there was no response, only the hollow echo of his despair. Frantically, Ethan searched the area, combing through the rain-drenched ruins, desperately hoping to find any trace of his beloved sister. But all he found were the fading footprints they had left behind, now slowly being washed away by the relentless downpour. In that bleak moment,

As reality set in, Ethan found himself standing on the precipice of a new chapter—one he'd have to traverse alone. Sarah's absence loomed like a shadow, a reminder of the bond they once shared. Gazing at the horizon, his heart ached with a mixture of grief and determination. The unknown stretched before him, a vast expanse he was now compelled to navigate without her reassuring presence.

Tears traced down his cheeks, their path mirroring the trails of uncertainty etched across his future. He closed his eyes, allowing the waves of sorrow to wash over him. In this moment of vulnerability, Ethan clenched his fists, his knuckles turning white with resolve. The promise he'd made to his sister echoed in his ears—the promise to journey onward, to pursue the enigmatic destination that was New Eden.

But as the weight of his sister's absence pressed upon him, a different path flickered in his thoughts. A path where he could set aside the search for a utopian city, where he could concentrate all his efforts on finding the one person he held most dear. The idea formed like a fragile whisper—an alternate route that begged for consideration.

He envisioned a life driven by the single-minded purpose of reuniting with Sarah, of scouring every corner of the decaying world for any trace of her. It was a quest fueled by the belief that she was still out there, lost but not gone. A journey that would require him to become a beacon of resilience, traversing the ruins with eyes that never wavered from their search.

With his heart heavy but resolute, Ethan stood at a crossroads. The pull of the journey to New Eden, the pursuit of hope for a world shrouded in darkness, tugged at him. But the ache for his sister, the desire to bring her back from the abyss, was equally compelling.

As he weighed these choices, he found himself back in the present moment. The breeze carried the scent of earth and decay, a reminder of the reality that surrounded him. His gaze shifted from the horizon to the skies, as if seeking guidance from the very stars that Sarah had once gazed upon with wonder.

With a deep breath, Ethan made his decision. The path he chose was not one of divergence, but of fusion. A path where the pursuit of New Eden and the search for his sister coexisted—a journey where each step he took held the potential to uncover both answers and solace.

The tears remained, but they now held a different meaning. They were not just tears of sorrow, but of determination. As they mingled with the earth beneath his feet, Ethan's resolve solidified. He would honor Sarah's memory not by leaving behind their shared mission, but by intertwining it with his new quest to reclaim what had been lost.

At that moment, he found strength—a strength that emanated from his sister's memory, a strength that fueled his steps forward. He wiped away his tears, the echoes of his vow resounding in the quiet of his heart. With newfound purpose, he set forth into the unknown, ready to confront the challenges that awaited and to bring back the light that had been lost.

He searches every broken building, every derelict alleyway, hoping to uncover even the smallest trace of his sister's presence. With each step, his heart pounds with a mix of hope and fear. He questions the few survivors he encounters, their weary faces reflecting the hardships they have endured. He listens intently, hanging onto every word, hoping they may have seen or heard something that could guide him.

But the wasteland keeps its secrets tightly guarded, offering no solace or answers. Ethan's hands grow calloused as he pushes aside debris, his eyes scanning for any sign of his sister. He searches their former hideouts, their childhood spots, places where they had sought solace amidst the chaos. The remnants of their shared existence taunt him with memories that are both comforting and agonizing. The once vibrant neighborhood now stands as a testament to the world's decay.

Crumbling buildings and broken infrastructure bear witness to the ravages of time and the relentless struggle for survival. Ethan moves through this desolation with a sense of urgency, as though time is slipping through his fingers, stealing away the chance to find Sarah. With each passing day, Ethan's determination grows stronger. He never wavers in his resolve to bring his sister back, no matter the challenges that lie ahead. The harsh reality of their world only fuels his determination, pushing him to endure exhaustion, hunger, and the constant threat of danger.

As the sun sets, casting long shadows across the desolate landscape, Ethan's searches continue, his flashlight cutting through the darkness. His heart aches with worry, his thoughts consumed by memories of Sarah's smile, her laughter, and their unbreakable bond. He clings to the hope that he will find her, that they will be reunited once again. Yet, despite his tireless efforts, the wasteland remains silent. The only sounds are the rustling of debris and the distant howling of the wind.

But Ethan refuses to give up. He knows that Sarah is out there somewhere, waiting to be found. With each passing day, Ethan's worry intensifies, gnawing at his heart like a relentless predator. The weight of uncertainty bears down on him heavily, driving him to retrace the familiar paths he and Sarah once walked together. His footsteps echo through the empty streets, each sound amplified by the absence of life.

Ethan visits their favorite hangouts, hoping for a miracle—a small clue, a whisper in the wind that would lead him to his sister's whereabouts. His eyes scan every nook and cranny, searching for any sign, any trace of Sarah's presence. The once vibrant corners they frequented now stand as empty reminders of happier times, the memories threatening to consume him. Determined not to confine his search to their neighborhood, Ethan expands his exploration into the more treacherous and unpredictable parts of the decaying city.

He navigates through crumbling buildings and hazardous alleys, his senses on high alert. Each step forward feels like a battle won against the ever-encroaching darkness. Hostile survivors and remnants of a crumbling society present constant threats, but Ethan refuses to be deterred. With gritted teeth and an unwavering resolve, he faces these challenges head-on. Each encounter tests his courage and resilience, but he fights with everything he has, driven by a fierce determination to find his sister.

The decaying city becomes a labyrinth of danger, demanding Ethan's unwavering focus and resourcefulness. He learns to anticipate the lurking dangers, developing a keen survival instinct. Each encounter becomes a battle of wits and strength as he navigates through the shadows, avoiding traps and overcoming obstacles that stand in his way. Exhaustion weighs on him, both physically and mentally, but he refuses to succumb to weariness. The urgency to find Sarah propels him forward, pushing him beyond his limits. His body aches, muscles protesting with every step, but he presses on, his sister's image etched firmly in his mind.

Along his journey, Ethan's relentless pursuit of his sister leads him to an underground network of survivors who have experienced similar losses. In this hidden enclave, he encounters a man named Jacob, a weathered and hardened survivor who has dedicated himself to unraveling the mysteries of the abductors. Jacob, scarred by his tragedy, becomes a beacon of hope and guidance for Ethan. With a sense of urgency in his voice, he shares his knowledge about the notorious group responsible for the abductions. His words carry a weight of experience and pain, resonating deeply with Ethan's fears and determination. Jacob explains that the abductors are a faction known as The Shadows, a clandestine organization that preys upon vulnerable survivors to exploit their skills or ransom them for resources. They operate under the cover of darkness, leaving little trace of their actions. Fear and uncertainty shroud their true motives, making them a formidable and elusive adversary.

As Jacob recounts stories of the abductors' ruthlessness and the horrors endured by their captives, Ethan's resolve strengthens. He sees the anguish in Jacob's eyes and recognizes the shared pain they both carry. Bound by a common purpose, they form an unspoken pact to bring an end to the reign of The Shadows and rescue those who have been taken. Under Jacob's guidance, Ethan delves deeper into the secrets surrounding The Shadows.

Hand in hand, they embark on an arduous quest, piecing together fragments of a puzzle woven from the aftermath of countless abductions. Their days become a dance of determination and discovery, as they methodically trace the elusive trails that the abductors leave in their wake. Every footstep takes them deeper into a shadowy labyrinth, and every whispered hint becomes a spark of hope igniting their resolve.

Amid stacks of maps and old scrolls, they huddle together, analyzing the faintest marks and symbols. Their fingers trace the inked lines that crisscross continents, leading them to forgotten corners of the world. Each map tells a story of a journey undertaken by those who sought the truth before them, leaving behind a cartographic breadcrumb trail that they now follow.

Surveillance footage plays like a silent movie, revealing snippets of the abductors' movements. The flicker of shadows and the faint gleam of moonlight offer glimpses into their methodology. Faces obscured by hoods, gestures shrouded in secrecy—it's a cryptic dance that they decode frame by frame.

Amid their research, a survivor's whispered rumor becomes a thread they dare not overlook. In hushed conversations around flickering campfires, survivors speak of eerie encounters and unsettling sights. Their words are laden with equal parts fear and determination, painting a picture of the abductors' elusiveness.

Amid the grind of their investigation, their determination to rescue Sarah remains unshaken. The weight of each discovery propels them forward, igniting a fire of anticipation that can only be quenched by the truth. In a world fractured by chaos, they unite in their pursuit, driven by the belief that the power of unity and resilience can prevail even against the darkest odds.

As the campfire crackled and cast dancing shadows, Ethan, Jacob, and a group of survivors huddled together, their faces illuminated by the warm glow.

Ethan leaned in, his eyes reflecting a mix of determination and exhaustion. "We need every lead we can find. Anything that could point us to where they might be holding Sarah."

Jacob nodded, his expression mirroring Ethan's intensity. "Agreed. We've been tracking their movements, piecing together patterns. But we need more. We need that one breakthrough that'll lead us straight to them."

A woman among the survivors cleared her throat, her voice carrying a hint of hesitation. "I've heard whispers, you know? Among other survivors. They talk about a place, hidden away. Some say it's a fortress, impenetrable. Others say it's a sanctuary, a haven."

Ethan's gaze sharpened as he absorbed her words. "Do you have a name? Any details about this place?"

The woman nodded, her eyes holding a mixture of fear and hope. "They call it 'The Veiled Sanctuary.' It's said to be deep in the heart of the ruins, cloaked by secrecy. People speak of strange symbols marking its entrance, symbols that seem to shift when you look away."

A man chimed in, his voice bearing the weight of experience. "I've heard tales of survivors who've stumbled upon it. Some were taken in, never to be seen again. Others... they returned, but changed. Like they'd been touched by something otherworldly."

Ethan exchanged a glance with Jacob, a silent understanding passing between them. "If there's even a chance that Sarah might be there, we have to investigate," Jacob stated firmly.

Ethan nodded in agreement, addressing the group. "We'll dig deeper into this Veiled Sanctuary. But remember, rumors can be as elusive as the truth. We'll need to approach this cautiously."

A survivor, a young man with a defiant spark in his eyes, spoke up. "We're with you, Ethan. We've seen what you've done, how you've united us. We won't let fear stop us."

The circle of survivors nodded in agreement, their faces a portrait of solidarity. At that moment, amidst the crackling fire and the backdrop of a world in turmoil, a collective determination took root—a shared conviction that they could overcome the odds stacked against them.

The underground network of survivors becomes Ethan's support system, offering resources, shelter, and invaluable knowledge. He forms bonds with other survivors, hearing their heart-wrenching stories of loss and their shared desire for justice. Together, they form a unified front against The Shadows, their collective resilience and determination becoming powerful.

As Ethan immerses himself in the treacherous world of The Shadows, he becomes intimately acquainted with their methods and tactics. He studies their patterns, analyzing their weaknesses and formulating strategies to outmaneuver them. Jacob becomes his mentor, imparting his hard-earned wisdom and combat skills, preparing Ethan for the impending confrontation. Through countless hours of planning, gathering intelligence, and honing their skills, Ethan and Jacob prepare for the dangerous and high-stakes mission to rescue Sarah and dismantle The Shadows.

Every step forward is fraught with anticipation and an ever-present sense of danger, but their shared determination refuses to waver. With their sights set on the abductors' stronghold, Ethan and Jacob gather a small team of trusted allies from the underground network. They equip themselves with weapons, ration supplies, and carefully devised rescue plans. The time for action has arrived, and their daring mission to confront The Shadows and save Sarah from their clutches is about to begin.

As Ethan delves deeper into the heart of the decaying city, he encounters remnants of a once-thriving civilization. Buildings stand as hollow shells, their walls covered in graffiti and their windows shattered. The eerie silence is broken only by the distant sound of the crumbling infrastructure and the occasional rustling of scavenging creatures. Navigating through treacherous alleyways and broken streets, Ethan's senses remain heightened. His every step is cautious, his eyes scanning the surroundings for any sign of danger.

The wasteland seems to whisper its secrets to him, guiding him toward the truth he seeks. As the chaos of the betrayal and ambush swirled around Ethan, his mind raced to find a way out of this dire situation. Amidst the confusion and the clash of swords, a single thought crystallized in his mind: New Eden held the key to reuniting with his sister. The memory of Sarah's disappearance resurfaced with painful clarity. He had promised himself that he would do whatever it took to find her, to keep her safe. Now, amid the chaos and deception, he knew that New Eden was his only chance to fulfill that promise.

CHAPTER FOUR

Captain Grace

Ethan's footsteps echoed through the desolate streets, each step punctuating the eerie silence that enveloped the decaying city. The sun cast long shadows over crumbling buildings and twisted metal, a haunting reminder of the world that once thrived here. As he cautiously surveyed his surroundings, his keen eyes caught a glimmer of movement near the outskirts. His curiosity piqued, Ethan's heart quickened its pace, adrenaline coursing through his veins. With caution etched into every line of his face, he approached the group of survivors huddled together near a makeshift camp. They stood in stark contrast to the disheveled and desperate individuals he had encountered thus far. A woman standing tall at the center of the group caught Ethan's attention. Her presence commanded authority and respect, her weathered face telling a story of hardships endured and battles fought. This was Captain Grace Thompson, a beacon of hope amidst the desolation.

As Ethan drew nearer, he noticed the careful organization and preparedness of the group. They had fortified their camp with salvaged materials, strategically placed sentries, and shared responsibilities. They possessed a sense of unity forged through shared struggles and the determination to survive. Captain Grace's piercing eyes, sharp and assessing, met Ethan's gaze. She observed him with a mix of skepticism and curiosity, weighing the risks and potential rewards of trusting a newcomer. Sensing the tension, Ethan tightened his grip on the worn blade hanging by his side, ready to defend himself if necessary. After a lingering silence,

Captain Grace's features softened, a flicker of recognition lighting up her eyes. She stepped forward, breaking the silence that hung heavy in the air.

"You there, newcomer," she called out, her voice steady yet tinged with caution. "State your name and your purpose in this forsaken place." Ethan squared his shoulders, meeting Captain Grace's gaze head-on. "I am Ethan Turner," he replied, his voice filled with determination. "I am searching for New Eden, a sanctuary rumored to hold the last flicker of hope for humanity. My father left me a message, guiding me towards it." Everyone in the camp burst out into laughter, aguy from the crowd shouted "last flicker of hope for humanity?" mocking him and continued laughing except Captain Grace. Captain Grace's eyes narrowed, scrutinizing Ethan's words and the resolve etched across his face. She recognized the same desperation and determination that had once fueled her quest for survival. After a moment of tense silence, Captain Grace's lips curved into a slight smile. It was a gesture of reluctant acceptance, a recognition of the potential she saw in Ethan's resilience. "Very well, Ethan Turner," she said, her voice laced with newfound trust. "You have my attention. Join us by the fire, and we shall discuss your quest for this fabled New Eden."

With that invitation, Ethan felt a wave of relief wash over him. He had found a kindred spirit in Captain Grace, someone who understood the harsh realities of their world and recognized the importance of holding onto hope. The path to New Eden seemed less treacherous now, with Captain Grace's guidance and the support of her resilient band of survivors. Captain Grace finally spoke, her voice softened slightly. "New Eden, huh?" Her eyes glistened with a mixture of skepticism and a flicker of hope. "It's a name that has circulated among the survivors. Some dismiss it as nothing more than a fairy tale, a figment of imagination born out of desperation. But to others, it represents a glimmer of hope—a possibility of something more." She paused for a moment, collecting her thoughts before continuing. "There have been whispers, murmurs carried by those who have ventured far and wide. They speak of a place untouched by the devastation, where life flourishes once again. A sanctuary where people have found refuge from the harsh realities of our world."

Captain Grace's voice carried a tinge of longing, a yearning for something beyond the grim existence they had grown accustomed to. "But I must be honest with you, Ethan. The rumors are just that—rumors. There's no concrete evidence, no guarantees. We are stepping into the unknown, placing our hopes in a place that may or may not exist." She met Ethan's gaze, her eyes reflecting a mix of caution and determination. "Yet, sometimes hope is all we have. It's what keeps us going in this desolate world. So, we'll chase this glimmer of hope and navigate the uncertainties together." Ethan felt a surge of gratitude washes over him, a weight lifting from his weary shoulders. The encounter with Captain Grace had given him renewed hope, a sense of purpose that he hadn't felt in a long time. In her weathered face and steady gaze, he saw a reflection of the harsh realities they both knew too well. Captain Grace had survived countless trials in this unforgiving wasteland. Her scars, both visible and hidden, bore witness to the battles fought and the losses endured. She possessed a deep understanding of the dangers lurking in the decaying city and the surrounding wasteland—knowledge that would prove invaluable in their search for New Eden. With Captain Grace by his side, Ethan's chances of reaching the rumored utopia increased tenfold. Her experience would guide them through treacherous paths, avoid pitfalls, and help them navigate the complex web of threats that awaited them.

As Captain Grace called her group together, Ethan stood among the survivors, taking in their weathered faces and determined expressions. Each person had a story etched into their features—a testament to the hardships they had endured. Their eyes held a glimmer of hope, a desperate yearning for a better life. Introductions were made, and Ethan learned about the individuals who would accompany him on this perilous journey. There was Jake, a seasoned fighter with a scar across his cheek—a reminder of countless battles fought. Sophie was a skilled tracker with a quiet strength that belied her petite frame. Ryan is a young man who had lost his family but refused to let despair consume him, fueled by an unwavering determination to find New Eden. And there were others, each possessing their unique skills and stories that had brought them to this moment.

Under Captain Grace's guidance, they began preparing for the challenges ahead. They gathered supplies, replenished their dwindling stock, and shared knowledge and strategies gleaned from their individual experiences. The camp came alive with a sense of purpose, their collective determination driving them forward. Maps were studied, routes debated, and plans laid out meticulously. Captain Grace, a seasoned leader, ensured that each member understood their roles and responsibilities. She emphasized the importance of unity and cooperation, acknowledging that their chances of survival relied on their ability to support one another. Ethan, his resolve solidified by the support and camaraderie he witnessed among the group, felt a renewed sense of purpose. He saw in each survivor a determination to overcome the bleakness of their surroundings. They all shared a common goal—to reach New Eden and find sanctuary, not just for themselves but for all those who had been affected by the devastation of the world.

As the sun set on their camp, casting a golden glow over their preparations, Ethan looked around at his newfound companions. They were a resilient and diverse group, bound together by the belief that a better future awaited them beyond the wasteland. With Captain Grace leading the way and Ethan's unwavering determination, they set their sights on the horizon, ready to face the treacherous journey ahead. The band of survivors united in purpose, began their trek toward the elusive New Eden. They moved cautiously and determined, navigating through dangerous terrain and avoiding threats lurking in the shadows. Each step brought them closer to their shared destination, their spirits bolstered by the strength of their collective will.

CHAPTER FIVE

The Scientist's Revelation

The band of survivors trudged through the rugged terrain, their determination unyielding despite the physical and emotional toll the journey had taken. Each step brought them closer to their destination—New Eden—a place that seemed like a distant dream, shrouded in uncertainty. As the group sought refuge in an abandoned structure, Ethan noticed a faint glimmer of light coming from a room down the corridor. Intrigued, he approached cautiously, his heart pounding with a mix of apprehension and hope. Pushing open the creaking door, he found himself in a dimly lit laboratory. Before him stood Dr. Samuel Collins, a figure enveloped in a worn lab coat. Ethan's eyes widened as he recognized the brilliance in the scientist's gaze. He had heard whispers of Dr. Collins—the last surviving genius in a world on the brink of collapse.

Captain Grace cleared her throat, her voice echoing in the dimly lit room, breaking the heavy silence that had settled among the survivors. Dr. Collins, deeply engrossed in his research, looked up with a start, his tired eyes widening as he registered the presence of the group. He studied them intently, his gaze shifting from one face to another, each displaying a unique mix of determination and weariness. "Dr. Collins, we have someone who seeks your guidance," Captain Grace announced, her voice carrying a note of urgency laced with hope. The scientist's weary expression transformed into a mix of curiosity and intrigue as his gaze settled on Ethan. His eyes flickered with recognition, the weariness momentarily lifted as a spark of interest ignited within him.

"Ah, another seeker of New Eden," Dr. Collins mused, his voice tinged with a hint of weariness that echoed the challenges he had witnessed throughout his journey. "I must admit, I never expected so many to brave the wasteland in search of salvation." Ethan stood before Dr. Collins, his youthful face filled with a determined resolve. He knew that in the presence of the brilliant scientist, he had a chance to uncover the truth about New Eden. The weight of his quest and the dreams of many survivors rested heavily on his shoulders.

"I come seeking answers, guidance," Ethan replied, his voice steady despite the uncertainty that lurked within. "My father left me a message, leading me to believe that New Eden holds the key to a brighter future. I seek to find it, to find hope for humanity." Dr. Collins leaned back in his chair; his fingers steepled together as he considered Ethan's words. His gaze held a mixture of wisdom and skepticism, a reflection of the countless obstacles he had encountered during his search for New Eden. "New Eden," Dr. Collins motioned for Ethan to take a seat, gesturing towards a worn-out chair. "Sit, my young friend," he said, his voice gentle yet laden with a sense of urgency. "There is much to discuss." As Ethan settled into the chair, the weight of anticipation hung heavy in the air. Dr. Collins, with a thoughtful expression etched on his face, began to paint a vivid picture of the state of Earth, revealing the harsh reality that had befallen their world. "Once, our planet teemed with life," Dr. Collins began, his voice tinged with a mixture of sorrow and determination. "But the unchecked greed and relentless pursuit of progress brought us to the brink of destruction. Pollution choked our skies, toxic chemicals contaminated our waters, and the land suffered from the relentless exploitation of its resources."

He paused for a moment, his eyes distant as he recalled the horrors of the past. "The consequences were devastating. Ecosystems collapsed, species perished, and the very foundation of life on Earth was eroded. The once-vibrant blue and green jewel we called home became a barren wasteland, where survival was a constant struggle." Ethan listened intently, his heart heavy with the weight of the truth. The image of a desolate Earth, stripped of its natural beauty, played vividly in his mind. However, Dr. Collins continued amidst the bleakness, his voice infused with a flicker of hope. "In the face of this impending doom, a group of visionary scientists dedicated their lives to finding a solution—a sanctuary where the last remnants of humanity could find solace and a chance at rebuilding a better future."

He leaned forward, his eyes shining with a mixture of passion and determination. "New Eden, as it came to be known, is the result of their tireless efforts. It is a sanctuary carefully constructed and hidden away from the rest of the world, a place where the lessons of the past can be learned from and a sustainable future can be forged." Ethan felt a surge of hope welling up within him. The thought of a place where humanity could start anew, where the mistakes of the past could be rectified, stirred something deep within his soul. "These visionary scientists sought to create not just a physical refuge but a haven for knowledge and innovation," Dr. Collins continued, his voice resonating with conviction. "Within the walls of New Eden, advanced technologies were developed, harnessing renewable energy sources and sustainable practices. It became a beacon of hope, a symbol that humanity still could rise even in the face of ruin."

Ethan absorbed every word, his mind racing with the possibilities that lay ahead. He realized that New Eden represented more than just a distant utopia—it was a chance for humanity to rediscover its potential and rebuild a society that valued balance and harmony with the planet. As Dr. Collins concluded his revelations, Ethan sat in awe of the immense undertaking that had gone into the creation of New Eden. The dire state of Earth became even more apparent, but so too did the glimmer of hope that New Eden offered. The path ahead would be treacherous, filled with obstacles and uncertainties. But armed with the knowledge imparted by Dr. Collins, Ethan knew that he had a duty to find New

Eden, not just for himself, but for the survival and redemption of humanity.

Ethan nodded, his heart swelling with gratitude for Dr. Collins' invaluable guidance. The scientist's warm smile and a glimmer of optimism filled him with renewed determination. "Thank you, Dr. Collins," Ethan said sincerely, his voice filled with genuine appreciation. "Your knowledge and guidance mean the world to me." Dr. Collins's eyes sparkled with pride and reassurance. "You have the strength and resilience to face the challenges ahead, Ethan," he affirmed. "I believe in you." Ethan rejoined Captain Grace and the group of survivors. Gathered around a worn-out table, they meticulously spread out the map provided by Dr. Collins. The aged parchment held the marks of time, its edges frayed and corners folded, bearing the weight of countless journeys taken.

Ethan traced his fingers along the faded ink lines, his eyes locked on the detailed markings that indicated treacherous territories, hidden paths, and potential havens along the way. The map revealed a daunting route, filled with danger and uncertainty, but it also held the key to unlocking a brighter future. As they studied the map together, their plan of action began to take shape. Captain Grace's experience and strategic mind proved invaluable as she led the discussion. The group considered the best route to follow, taking into account the hazards they would encounter and the need to avoid hostile factions that lurked in the wasteland. Their voices filled the room as they deliberated, each member sharing their insights and concerns.

Together, they developed a comprehensive plan, their fingers tracing paths on the map as they discussed safe zones, possible detours, and potential obstacles. They strategized ways to stay under the radar, avoiding the attention of marauders and rival factions that sought to exploit the remnants of a broken world. Captain Grace's authoritative voice brought their planning session to a close. "We have our course," she declared, her gaze sweeping across the group. "Stay vigilant, stick together, and remember our objective—New Eden." Each member of the group possessed unique skills and experiences that would prove vital in their journey toward the fabled utopia. They were a collective force bound by a shared purpose and the belief in a brighter future.

CHAPTER SIX

Lessons from Marcus

After their encounter with Dr. Samuel Collins, Ethan, and his newfound companions embark on their journey toward the fabled utopia of New Eden. The decaying cityscape stretched out before them, a bleak reminder of the world they were leaving behind. As they made their way through the desolate streets, Ethan couldn't help but feel a sense of trepidation. The gravity of their mission weighed heavily on his shoulders, and doubts crept into his mind. Would they truly find salvation in New Eden, or was it just a figment of their imagination? It was during one particularly grueling day of travel that Ethan first met Marcus Reed. They had stumbled upon an old abandoned building, seeking shelter from an approaching storm. Little did Ethan know that these chance encounters would change the course of his journey.

In the dim light of the dilapidated structure, Marcus emerged from the shadows. His weathered face and piercing eyes betrayed a life in the harshest conditions. There was an air of wisdom and experience that surrounded him, drawing Ethan's curiosity. "Looks like you folks could use a helping hand," Marcus said, his voice a low rumble. Ethan, Captain Grace, and Dr. Collins exchanged wary glances before Ethan stepped forward. "Who are you? How do you know we need help?" he asked, his voice tinged with caution. Marcus chuckled, a sound that echoed through the desolate building. "Call it a gut feeling, young man. I've been watching you all from a distance. The world outside these walls is a dangerous place, and I figured you could use someone who knows the ropes."

Curiosity mixed with desperation compelled Ethan to listen to what Marcus had to offer. He recognized the value of experience in this unforgiving world, and the prospect of a seasoned guide was too enticing to ignore. With a nod from Captain Grace, Ethan extended his hand to Marcus. "I'm Ethan. We're on our way to New Eden, searching for hope. Can you truly help us?" Marcus grasped Ethan's hand firmly, his gaze unwavering. "Ethan, I can't guarantee anything, but I've seen enough in my time to know a thing or two about survival. If you're willing to listen and learn, I'll do my best to guide you through the dangers that lie ahead."

As Ethan and Marcus continued their trek through the decaying city, Marcus began to share his own survival stories, drawing Ethan into a world of danger, perseverance, and hope. They found themselves in an area of the city where towering skyscrapers once stood. The skeletal remains of these structures cast long shadows over the desolate streets, a haunting reminder of the city's former glory. Marcus gestured toward one particularly tall building that had miraculously held together despite the ravages of time. "I spent weeks holed up in that building," Marcus said, his voice tinged with a mix of nostalgia and sadness. "There were others with me back then, survivors like us. We pooled our resources and rationed our supplies, hoping for a chance to escape this forsaken place." As they cautiously entered the building, Marcus recounted the trials they faced. He spoke of the desperate search for food and water, of the constant fear of being discovered by rival factions or predatory scavengers. He detailed the nights spent huddled together, listening to the distant echoes of unrest and violence that plagued the city.

"We had to learn how to make the best of what we had," Marcus continued, his eyes scanning the dimly lit surroundings. "We scoured every floor for supplies, using our knowledge of the building's layout to our advantage. We created makeshift traps and barricades to keep intruders at bay." Ethan listened intently, his imagination bringing the harrowing tales to life. Marcus's stories painted vivid pictures of survival and resilience in the face of unimaginable hardships. He described moments of desperation but also moments of triumph and unexpected kindness. "There was this one time," Marcus began with a smile, "when we stumbled upon an old storage room that had been overlooked by others. It was like finding a treasure trove. We found cans of food, clean water, and even some medical supplies. It was a small victory, but it gave us hope."

Ethan could feel the weight of those experiences, the resilience, and determination that had carried Marcus through the darkest of times. It was in those moments that Marcus's mentorship truly began to take root within Ethan's heart. Marcus went on to teach Ethan about the importance of reading the signs and signals left behind by others who had passed through the city before them. He showed him how to decipher graffiti, markings, and even the patterns of debris left behind. These seemingly random remnants held valuable information about potential dangers and hidden caches of supplies. As they exited the building, Marcus paused and pointed to a faded symbol spray-painted on the side of a wall. "That symbol," he said, "signifies a safe house established by a group of survivors. They would provide refuge, food, and a sense of community. Keep an eye out for these symbols, (he points at a symbol of a camel), Ethan. They may just save your life one day."

As Ethan and Marcus ventured through the desolate streets of the decaying city, Marcus began imparting his survival skills with a meticulousness that reflected his years of experience. He led Ethan through narrow alleyways, avoiding open spaces that left them vulnerable to potential threats. With each step, Marcus pointed out potential dangers, such as loose debris, hidden crevices, and unstable structures. They approached a particularly dilapidated building, its walls crumbling and roof on the verge of collapse. Marcus halted and motioned for Ethan to do the same. With a cautionary tone, he explained, "Always assess the stability of the structures we encounter. Look for signs of decay, cracks, or sagging beams. Our lives depend on making wise choices." Ethan watched intently as Marcus demonstrated how to test the stability of the building. He gently prodded the walls, listened for creaks or groans, and studied the patterns of cracks. Marcus explained the importance of avoiding areas prone to collapse and advised Ethan to always have an exit strategy in mind when entering any structure.

Moving forward, Marcus taught Ethan the art of moving silently and stealthily through their environment. He emphasized the need for silence to avoid drawing unwanted attention from other survivors or potential threats. They practiced walking softly, avoiding loose debris, and using the surrounding structures as cover to mask their movements. As they continued their journey, Marcus shared stories of past encounters and the valuable lessons he had learned from them. He recounted instances of narrowly escaping scavenger gangs, evading deadly traps set by desperate survivors, and surviving encounters with dangerous wildlife that now roamed the desolate streets. Ethan listened intently, absorbing Marcus' words like a sponge, understanding the importance of learning from the experiences of those who had come before him. In one particularly dangerous area, Marcus led Ethan to a hidden cache of supplies, cleverly concealed beneath a pile of rubble. With a smile, he explained the significance of resourcefulness and adaptability in their harsh world. He taught Ethan to search for hidden stashes and to salvage useful items from the wreckage around them. "Sometimes, survival means finding the strength to see opportunity amidst the ruins," Marcus remarked.

With each passing day, Ethan's confidence grew. He became adept at spotting potential dangers, navigating treacherous terrain, and evading potential threats. Marcus took note of Ethan's progress, encouraging him and offering guidance whenever necessary. He reminded Ethan that survival wasn't just about physical prowess but also about mental resilience and adaptability. Marcus brought their lesson to a close as the sun dipped below the horizon, casting an eerie glow over the desolate landscape. They found a secluded spot to rest, where Marcus sat down with Ethan by his side. Looking into Ethan's eyes, he said, "Remember, survival is not just about staying alive; it's about holding onto hope and retaining your humanity amidst the chaos. We carry the responsibility to build a better world for those who come after us." Ethan nodded, gratitude evident in his eyes. He had found not only a mentor in Marcus but also a guiding light in the darkness.

Ethan and Marcus traversed the cityscape, encountering both the expected dangers and unexpected moments of camaraderie. Marcus shared more stories of survival and resilience, painting a vivid picture of the world before it crumbled into chaos. He spoke of the diverse communities that once thrived within the city, the vibrant streets filled with laughter and dreams. Ethan listened intently, absorbing the tales of a world long lost, a world he could only imagine through Marcus's words. One evening, as they took shelter in an abandoned building, Marcus gazed out at the starless sky, a somber expression on his weathered face. "I remember a time when the nights were filled with twinkling stars," he said wistfully. "We could look up and dream of reaching those distant lights, of exploring the vastness of the universe. Now, the night sky serves as a constant reminder of the world we've lost."

Ethan felt a pang of sadness as he observed the weary lines etched on Marcus's face. He realized that Marcus, like many others, had carried the weight of their shattered world for far too long. Ethan spoke up, determined to lift the heaviness from his mentor's shoulders. "Marcus, even though the stars are hidden from us now, we still have hope. We're on a journey to find New Eden, a place where your dreams may still be within reach. We can forge a new path that brings light back into our lives." Marcus's gaze shifted from the darkened sky to Ethan's hopeful eyes. A glimmer of a smile played on his lips. "You're right, Ethan. Our journey to New Eden is more than just a search for physical sanctuary. It's a quest to reclaim our dreams and rebuild a world worth living in. With each step we take, we breathe life back into the possibility of a brighter future."

Encouraged by their shared resolve, Ethan and Marcus pressed on, their spirits lifted by the belief that their mission was more significant than mere survival. They encountered remnants of the past, moments that stirred memories and hope. In the ruins of a once-thriving marketplace, Ethan discovered a faded mural depicting scenes of unity and diversity—a poignant reminder of the world they longed to create. As they traveled deeper into the heart of the decaying city, they encountered other survivors along the way. Some sought refuge, while others shared valuable knowledge about hidden paths and sources of sustenance. Through these interactions, Ethan witnessed the power of human connection amidst the ruins. Strangers became allies, banding together to support one another on this arduous journey toward New Eden.

One evening, as they rested beneath the remnants of a crumbling bridge, Marcus gathered the group together. Ethan, Marcus, and Dr. Collins formed a circle, their eyes fixed on their mentor figure. "We've come a long way," Captain Grace began, her voice steady and filled with purpose. "And I've seen each of you grow stronger and more resilient with every challenge we've faced. But our journey is not over yet. The path to New Eden is treacherous, and the obstacles ahead will test our resolve. However, as long as we remain united, as long as we hold onto hope and trust in one another, we will overcome whatever lies in our way." Her words echoed in the hearts of his companions, fueling their determination. They nodded in agreement, understanding that they were bound not just by their shared destination but by the bonds forged through adversity. They had become a family in this broken world that would fight for a future where hope, compassion, and the dreams of a better tomorrow could flourish once again.

They knew that the road ahead would not be easy and sacrifices needed to be made, but their belief in a brighter future burned brightly within their hearts. As they resumed their journey, the city seemed to whisper secrets of its past, the stories of those who had come before. Each crumbling building, each silent street, held remnants of lives lived and dreams unfulfilled. But Ethan and his companions pressed on, guided by the lessons learned from Marcus. They moved with a quiet determination, understanding that their steps were not just for themselves but for the countless others who yearned for a second chance.

And so, beneath the ash-laden sky, Ethan and his resilient band of survivors ventured forth, fueled by the unshakeable hope that lay within them. The road to New Eden stretched before them, challenging their resilience and testing their spirits, but they knew they were not alone. They carried the memories and teachings of Marcus Reed, their mentor, guide, and beacon of hope in this desolate world. With Marcus's wisdom echoing in their minds, they stepped into the unknown, united in their shared quest for a lost horizon where dreams could be reborn. Little did they know that their encounter with Marcus Reed was just the beginning of an extraordinary journey that would shape their destinies, test their limits, and ignite a rebellion against the corrupt regime that awaited them in the fractured society of New Eden.

CHAPTER SEVEN

The Journey

Ethan and his newfound companions gathered their meager supplies and set out toward New Eden, their hearts filled with hope and determination. The weight of their mission bore down upon them, but they refused to let despair consume their spirits. They knew that the journey ahead would be filled with uncertainty and danger, yet they pressed on, driven by the promise of a better future. As they navigated through the decaying city, remnants of a once-vibrant civilization surrounded them. The crumbling infrastructure and dilapidated buildings stood as solemn reminders of humanity's fall from grace. The once bustling streets were now eerie and desolate, with a haunting stillness that sent shivers down their spines. The only illumination came from the fading sunlight that filtered through the thick layers of smog and dust, casting an otherworldly glow over the desolate landscape. Shadows danced and twisted among the ruins, their movements hinting at the lurking dangers that awaited them.

Every step they took was a gamble, as hidden pitfalls and unstable debris threatened to bring them crashing down. Their senses heightened; they moved with caution, their eyes scanning their surroundings for any signs of danger. The ruins had become a haven for bandits and lawless factions, their predatory instincts honed by the harsh realities of this forsaken world. They relied on their wits and instincts to navigate through the treacherous terrain. Crumbling buildings loomed like skeletal remains, their structural integrity teetering on the brink of collapse. Each carefully calculated step took them through a maze of debris and obstacles, the remnants of a society that had succumbed to its hubris. The sound of their footsteps echoed through the desolation, a constant reminder of their vulnerability. They remained vigilant, always on guard, as the ruins whispered tales of danger and betrayal. Every corner turned, every shadow cast, held the potential for an ambush or a deadly confrontation. Their journey became a test of both physical endurance and mental fortitude. They faced harsh weather conditions, scorching sun during the day, and bone-chilling cold at night. Their provisions dwindled, forcing them to make difficult choices and ration their supplies. Hunger gnawed at their stomachs, and thirst parched their throats, but they pressed on, fueled by their shared determination. Yet, amidst the desolation and danger, a bond began to form between the companions. They found solace in each other's presence, drawing strength from their shared purpose. Encouragement and support became the pillars that held them together, even in the face of adversity.

As they continued their arduous trek through the wasteland, Ethan and his companions encountered a diverse array of survivors, each with their own stories and reasons for venturing towards New Eden. The meeting of these individuals brought both challenges and unexpected moments of connection. One survivor they encountered was Jenna, a young woman who had learned to fend for herself in the harsh realities of the post-apocalyptic world. Her eyes carried a hint of caution, evidence of the hardships she had faced. Initially distrustful of the group, Jenna eventually found solace in their shared journey and joined them, seeking the hope and security that New Eden represented. Among the survivors was also Camill, an elderly man who had lost his family during the chaos that consumed the world. Despite his age, Camill possessed a resilience that was forged through the trials he had endured. With a gentle demeanor and a wealth of wisdom, he became a source of guidance and comfort for those who were struggling to find their place in the desolate landscape.

Another survivor, Sofia, was a skilled archer who had honed her abilities to protect herself from the dangers that lurked outside the city walls. Her piercing gaze and quiet determination revealed the strength that lay within her. Sofia had carried the weight of her past losses, but the camaraderie she found in Ethan's group allowed her to open up. Each evening, as they made camp amidst the ruins, the survivors would gather around the crackling fire, seeking warmth and companionship. They shared their personal stories, the memories of their past lives that served as a reminder of what they had lost. The tales were often tinged with sorrow, but they also held sparks of hope for a brighter future.

Mia, a young girl with wild, untamed hair and a resilient spirit, had managed to retain her youthful innocence despite the harsh realities of their world. Her wide eyes absorbed every story with awe and wonder, finding solace in the tales of bravery and resilience. She became a beacon of innocence and optimism, reminding the group of the importance of hope in the face of despair. Daniel, a skilled mechanic, brought a practical and resourceful mindset to the group. With his knack for repairing and repurposing technology, he ensured that their meager supplies lasted longer and their makeshift vehicles remained operational. His technical expertise was crucial to their survival in the unforgiving environment they traversed. Through the shared stories, laughter, and occasional tears, the survivors forged bonds of friendship and camaraderie.

Amidst the cluster of survivors, where flickering campfires cast wavering shadows, a poignant scene unfolded. In the corner of the group, nestled within the circle of weary souls, stood a little girl. Her eyes shimmered with a delicate blend of disbelief and joy, her tear-streaked cheeks reflecting the dancing flames. It was a sight that stopped time, a moment of stark contrast against the backdrop of despair.

Among the murmurs of gratitude and relief that echoed through the makeshift camp, a whispered name rippled through the air like a tender breeze—Sarah. The same sister whom Ethan had longed to reunite with, now stood before him, wrapped in the arms of survival. In her eyes, happiness mingled with the hardships she had endured, a testament to the resilience of a child who had navigated the same harsh realities as the rest.

For Ethan, the sight was a jolt of unanticipated emotion. His heart swelled with a blend of disbelief, relief, and an overwhelming rush of protective tenderness. His little sister, who had been a beacon of hope throughout his journey, stood before him, her very presence affirming that the path he had chosen was the right one.

As their gazes locked, the distance and danger that had separated them for so long felt like distant memories. In Sarah's eyes, he glimpsed a reflection of his own determination, mirrored in her unwavering strength. In that fragile moment, amidst the ruins and the rubble, they found an unexpected reunion—a testament to the enduring power of family, and a glimmer of light amid the darkness that surrounded them.

They found strength in one another, supporting each other through the darkest moments of their journey. The weight of Ethan's responsibility became more bearable as he witnessed the resilience and determination in his companions' eyes.

Doubt and fatigue gnawed at their spirits, threatening to extinguish the flickering flame of hope that had sustained them throughout their journey. The arduous trek through the decaying city and the constant trials they faced had taken their toll. But they refused to yield. Their determination burned brighter than ever as they pushed forward, driven by the unwavering belief that New Eden held the answers they sought. Their weary legs propelled them onward, step by step, through the unforgiving wasteland. The once-distant walls of New Eden loomed larger with each passing mile, rising like an impenetrable fortress against the desolate backdrop. A mix of awe and trepidation filled their hearts as they realized the enormity of the challenge ahead. The sight of the towering walls inspired a sense of wonder and possibility, but it also evoked a sense of unease. What mysteries lay hidden within those formidable barriers? What secrets did New Eden hold? The group exchanged glances, silently acknowledging the unspoken questions that swirled in their minds.

As they approached the threshold of the fabled utopia, a shiver of anticipation coursed through their weary bodies. They could almost taste the promise of a better life, of a sanctuary from the desolation that had consumed the world. Yet, the unknown lay before them like uncharted territory, stirring both excitement and trepidation. With bated breath, they halted just outside the walls of New Eden. The massive gates, adorned with intricate patterns and symbols, stood as the final barrier between them and their elusive sanctuary. The sun cast long shadows, stretching across the desolate landscape, as if emphasizing the gravity of their arrival. The scent of possibility hung heavy in the air, mingling with the dust of the wasteland. Their eyes scanned the walls, searching for any signs of life or movement within. But the silence was deafening, leaving them to wonder what awaited them on the other side. The anticipation was almost palpable, their hearts pounding in their chests. Ethan and his companions, though weary and battle-worn, stood tall and resolute. They had come too far to turn back now. With a shared nod of determination, they prepared to cross the threshold, ready to confront the realities that awaited them within the enigmatic city of New Eden.

Spread out below, the sprawling city of New Eden stretched as far as the eye could see, its towering structures reaching toward the heavens. Gleaming spires and pristine architecture contrasted starkly with the desolation of the wasteland. The city walls encircled the metropolis, creating a formidable barrier between the sanctuary within and the harsh realities of the outside world. The city was an oasis of life, a stark contrast to the barren wasteland that lay beyond its borders. Vibrant greenery and carefully cultivated gardens adorned the open spaces, offering a glimpse of nature's resilience. Parks and communal areas dotted the landscape, providing gathering spaces for the inhabitants.

It was a stark reminder of what humanity had lost but also a testament to their unwavering determination to create a semblance of normalcy in an unforgiving world. The centerpiece of New Eden was the towering citadel at its heart, a majestic structure that reached towards the sky. Its shimmering façade reflected the sunlight, creating a mesmerizing spectacle of light and color. Guard towers lined the perimeter, standing as silent sentinels, ever vigilant against the threats of the outside world. As Ethan gazed upon the grandeur of New Eden, a mix of awe and uncertainty filled his heart. The sight promised safety, stability, and a chance at a better life. But he couldn't shake off the nagging feeling that beneath the surface lay secrets and hidden truths that could shatter their illusions of paradise.

CHAPTER EIGHT

Betrayal and Ambush

As the gates of New Eden swung open, Ethan and his companions cautiously stepped inside, their eyes wide with a mixture of anticipation and unease. The cityscape within the walls appeared vastly different from the desolation they had left behind. Towers rose toward the heavens, their sleek, modern architecture standing in stark contrast to the crumbling ruins of the outside world. Gardens bloomed with vibrant colors, their sweet fragrance wafting through the air. The sound of laughter and conversation filled the streets, creating a symphony of life that seemed almost surreal to Ethan and his weary companions. They were welcomed with open arms by the citizens of New Eden, their faces beaming with contentment and their expressions unburdened by the hardships of the wasteland. People moved about with purpose, going about their daily lives with a sense of security and stability that Ethan had long forgotten. The sight of children playing in the parks, their laughter echoing through the air, brought a smile to his face, dispelling some of the darkness that had settled within his soul.

Ethan couldn't help but feel a flicker of optimism as he observed the harmonious coexistence of the citizens. It seemed that, against all odds, this utopia had managed to carve out a haven of peace and prosperity amidst the chaos of the outside world. A glimmer of hope ignited within him, fueling his resolve to find solace in this promised land. As they walked through the bustling streets, people greeted them warmly, offering assistance and kind words. Ethan marveled at the advanced technology and infrastructure that sustained the city. Clean energy sources powered the buildings, and the air was free from the acrid stench of pollution that had plagued the wasteland. The abundance of resources and the absence of struggle seemed almost too good to be true. New Eden's citizens shared stories of their past, recounting the hardships they had endured before finding sanctuary within these walls. Their narratives painted a picture of a society that had overcome adversity, united under a common vision for a better future. They spoke of harmony, cooperation, and progress, reaffirming Ethan's belief that he had finally found the refuge he had sought for so long.

Guided by Dr. Collins, Ethan, and his companions walked through the opulent halls of the central building, their footsteps echoing on the polished marble floors. The walls were adorned with grand tapestries and intricate artwork, depicting a prosperous society that seemed to exist in stark contrast to the desolation outside. As they approached the grand chamber, Ethan couldn't shake off a growing sense of unease. The tension in the air was palpable, like a thick fog that obscured the true intentions of those gathered within. He glanced at his companions, searching for reassurance in their expressions, but found only mirrored concern. Pushing open the heavy double doors, they stepped into the grand chamber, and the sight that greeted them was chilling. The room was filled not only with the leaders of New Eden but also with individuals Ethan did not recognize—a rival faction that had infiltrated the utopia's inner sanctum. Their eyes gleamed with malice and triumph, an unsettling contrast to the warm reception they had received upon their arrival.

Captain Grace and Marcus were conspicuously absent, their absence casting a shadow of doubt over the situation. Panic gripped Ethan's heart as realization dawned. They had walked directly into a trap, lured by the promise of salvation and manipulated by Dr. Collins, who had orchestrated this elaborate ruse. The sense of betrayal was overwhelming. Ethan had placed his trust in Dr. Collins, believing in the scientist's knowledge and intentions. He had seen him as an ally, a beacon of hope in this desolate world.

Now, that trust was shattered, replaced by a sense of vulnerability and anger.

The chamber fell into a tense silence as Ethan's gaze locked with Dr. Collins' eyes. There was guilt etched in the scientist's features, a flicker of remorse that offered little solace. It became clear that Dr. Collins' motivations were driven by ambition, a hunger for power, and control over the untapped potential of New Eden. The realization hit Ethan like a physical blow. He felt a mix of anger, disappointment, and profound sadness. How could someone they had relied upon and respected stoop so low? How could he have been so blind to the underlying deceit? The rival faction, emboldened by Dr. Collins' betrayal, revealed their true intentions—to exploit the newcomers for their gain. Their lust for power was palpable, their eyes filled with greed as they surveyed Ethan and his companions like commodities to be claimed. The room erupted into chaos as armed guards closed in, separating Ethan from his remaining allies. The group was outnumbered and outmatched, but a spark of defiance burned within Ethan's heart. He refused to succumb to the overwhelming odds.

Ethan's progress came to an abrupt halt as he found himself surrounded by guards. Their stern gazes locked onto him, their weapons held at the ready. Ethan's heart pounded in his chest, uncertainty mingling with the remnants of his anger and disappointment. Through the throng of guards, Dr. Collins emerged, his countenance heavy with guilt and regret. Ethan's eyes bore into the scientist's, demanding an explanation, an understanding of the motives behind his actions. A tense silence filled the air as Dr. Collins stepped forward, his voice carrying a mix of resignation and remorse.

"Ethan," he began, his tone tinged with a melancholic weight, "I never intended for it to come to this. But you must understand the potential within New Eden, the power it holds; I believe that I could guide and shape its destiny for the betterment of humanity." Dr. Collins' words hung in the air, heavy with the weight of his conflicting desires. Ethan's brows furrowed as he listened, a mix of confusion and lingering anger clouding his judgment. He yearned to comprehend the depths of Dr. Collins‘ betrayal, to uncover the true motivations that had driven him to such extremes. "I thought I could bring about change, that I could use the resources of New Eden to create a brighter future," Dr. Collins continued, his voice laced with a touch of desperation. "But I see now the error of my ways, the cost of my ambition. My actions have endangered not only you and your companions but the very ideals we sought to protect."

Ethan's eyes flickered with a mix of skepticism and a faint glimmer of understanding. He couldn't fully grasp the depth of Dr. Collins' choices, the internal struggle that had led him astray. The scientist's words resonated with a sense of remorse, but they did little to alleviate the pain and betrayal Ethan had experienced. Dr. Collins stepped closer, his gaze holding a mixture of regret and pleading. "Ethan, please understand that I am filled with remorse for the choices I have made. I wanted to believe that I could lead New Eden toward a brighter future, but in doing so, I lost sight of the values we once held dear. I betrayed not only you but also my convictions."

Ethan remained silent for a moment, his mind grappling with the conflicting emotions that swirled within. He knew that understanding Dr. Collins‘ motivations was the first step toward forgiveness, toward untangling the web of deception that had ensnared them all. But forgiveness would not come easily or swiftly. "You may have believed in a greater cause, Dr. Collins, but you manipulated us; you played with our lives," Ethan finally spoke, his voice laced with a mixture of disappointment and a hint of lingering trust. "Your remorse does not excuse for what you've done, the lives you've put at risk. I will seek the truth, not only for the sake of New Eden but for those who trusted you and suffered because of it." Dr. Collins' gaze dropped, a silent acknowledgment of his actions.

As Ethan was led through the dimly lit corridors of New Eden, his heart sank at the sight that awaited him in the depths of the prison. The heavy iron doors creaked open, revealing a cramped and cold cell. It was within these grim confines that he discovered Captain Grace and Marcus, their faces etched with exhaustion and resignation. A flicker of relief passed through Ethan at the sight of his companions, but it was swiftly overshadowed by the realization that their situation seemed dire and devoid of hope. The prison walls seemed to amplify the weight of their betrayal as if trapping them in a metaphorical cage of broken trust and shattered dreams.

Captain Grace's eyes met Ethan's, a glimmer of determination still present, though dimmed by their predicament. Her voice, once filled with authority and unwavering confidence, carried a tinge of weariness as she addressed him. "Ethan, it seems we find ourselves in a most unfortunate situation. Dr. Collins' betrayal has placed us all at the mercy of those who seek to exploit New Eden." Marcus, usually the embodiment of resilience and strength, leaned against the cold stone wall, his gaze distant and weary. His voice held a hint of bitterness as he spoke. "We were blind, Ethan. Blinded by our desperation for a better future, for the hope that New Eden promised. But hope can be a cruel illusion, a veil that hides the darker realities that lurk beneath." Ethan nodded solemnly, the weight of their words sinking deep into his core. The realization that they were trapped, not only physically within the prison walls but also in a web of deceit and manipulation, settled heavily upon him. The flicker of hope he had clung to was now shrouded in doubt and uncertainty.

CHAPTER NINE

The Underground Network

Ethan, Marcus, and Captain Grace found themselves shackled and herded alongside other prisoners, their eyes filled with defiance and a flicker of hope. The journey to the outside prison was long and arduous, the regime's guards showing no mercy as they pushed and taunted their captives. As they neared their destination, the desolate landscape came into view, a barren expanse that mirrored the inner decay of New Eden. Tall fences and imposing guard towers loomed in the distance, casting a shadow over the prisoners' spirits. It was here, amidst the unforgiving wilderness, that their paths would cross with the rebel leader, a figure known only through whispers and tales of resistance. Once inside the outer prison, the atmosphere grew even more oppressive. The guards tightened their grip on Ethan, Marcus, and Grace, wary of any sign of rebellion. But as they were led through the prison's cold corridors, their eyes met those of their fellow inmates, eyes that spoke of resilience and defiance. Finally, they were brought before a cell. The door creaked open, revealing a figure huddled in the shadows.

"Who are you?" Ethan mouthed the words, cautious yet filled with curiosity.

The man's face creased into a smile, lines etched deep with wisdom and countless battles fought. His eyes held the weight of his leadership, reflecting both the hardships he had endured and the unwavering resolve that propelled him forward. "Call me Alexander," he said, his voice steady and commanding. "I am the leader of the underground resistance against the tyrannical rule of New Eden." Ethan's heart skipped a beat, and a flicker of hope rekindled within him. Alexander's presence exuded strength and resilience, offering a glimmer of possibility amidst the bleakness of their captivity. He motioned for the others to gather closer, their eyes fixed on Alexander, anticipation mingling with a renewed sense of purpose. As they huddled together, Alexander began to share his story. He spoke of a childhood spent witnessing the corruption of the regime, the injustices inflicted upon innocent lives, and the hardships that had forged him into the leader he had become. He had faced numerous trials and tribulations, losing loved ones along the way, but his unwavering determination had never wavered.

With each word, Alexander painted a vivid picture of the resistance, the network of brave individuals who had dedicated their lives to challenging the status quo. He spoke of their ingenuity, their unwavering loyalty, and their willingness to sacrifice everything for the cause. They had infiltrated the darkest corners of New Eden, gathering vital information and waiting for the right moment to strike. Ethan listened intently, his admiration for Alexander growing with each passing moment. Here was a leader who had faced adversity head-on, inspiring others to rise against the oppressive regime. He embodied the resilience and spirit of the resistance, a symbol of hope for those who had long suffered under New Eden's rule.

Alexander's gaze met Ethan's, his eyes filled with both sorrow and determination. He leaned in closer, his voice lowering to a conspiratorial tone. "New Eden was not always the idyllic haven it claims to be," he began, his words laced with a mix of anger and sadness. "It was built upon the ruins of the old world, a façade to mask the darkness that lies within." Ethan's curiosity deepened, his heart pounding in anticipation of the truth. The pieces of the puzzle started to click into place, revealing a more complex reality behind the utopia they had believed in. He couldn't help but wonder how they had been blind to the deeper layers of corruption that tainted

New Eden's promise. Alexander took a steadying breath, his voice carrying the weight of years of uncovering the regime's secrets. "The leaders of New Eden manipulate the minds of its inhabitants, suppressing their free will and shaping their beliefs to maintain control. They hoard resources, leaving many in poverty and despair, while a privileged few thrive within the walls of their opulent palaces."

Ethan's breath caught in his throat, a mix of anger and disbelief swirling within him. The idealized vision of New Eden shattered before his eyes, replaced by a grim reality of exploitation and inequality. His desire to reach this utopia had been based on false hope, but now, armed with knowledge, he felt a renewed sense of purpose burning within him. "We aim to expose the truth, to liberate the people from the shackles of this false paradise," Alexander continued, his voice filled with resolve. "Together, we will show the world what New Eden truly is and spark a revolution that will shake the foundations of their corrupted society." Ethan's determination solidified, fueled by the injustice he had witnessed and the newfound knowledge of the regime's deception. The rebellion's cause had shifted from mere survival to fighting for the freedom of the countless souls held captive within the walls of New Eden.

With a firm nod, Ethan extended his hand toward Alexander, sealing their unspoken alliance. They were now part of something bigger than themselves, united in their cause to dismantle the corrupt regime, expose their lies, and restore freedom to New Eden. The door to their prison cell creaked open, revealing the silhouettes of the guards, but this time, Ethan and his newfound comrades stood tall, their spirits unbreakable. They were ready to face the challenges that lay ahead, knowing that together with Alexander and the resistance, they had a fighting chance. As the guards approached, their expressions etched with arrogance and superiority, Alexander's voice sliced through the tension-laden air. "Listen carefully," he said, his tone filled with authority. "We have a plan."

He proceeded to outline their escape strategy, detailing the intricate steps that would lead them to freedom. The rebel army had been meticulously preparing for this moment, and Alexander's leadership shone through as he explained each element of the plan with precision. Their first objective was to neutralize the guards and gain control of the prison block. Alexander assigned specific roles to each member of the group, utilizing their unique skills and expertise. Captain Grace would lead the assault, utilizing her strategic brilliance and combat prowess. Marcus, with his proficiency in stealth, would be responsible for disabling the security systems. Ethan's role as the newest member of the resistance was crucial. Alexander designated him as the catalyst, the spark that would ignite the rebellion within the hearts of their fellow prisoners. Ethan was to rally the captives, offering them hope and encouraging them to join the fight against their common oppressors. The plan was ambitious, but their determination burned bright. Alexander emphasized the importance of unity and discipline, urging each member of the group to rely on one another. Their success depended on the cohesion of the team and the unwavering belief in their shared cause. As Alexander finished outlining the plan, a renewed sense of purpose surged through Ethan and his comrades. They exchanged determined glances, a silent agreement that they would give their all for the rebellion and the freedom of New Eden. At that moment, they were more than just a group of individuals – they were a formidable force, ready to challenge the regime's grip on power.

As the guards grew nearer, their footsteps echoing ominously, Ethan took a deep breath. The time they had come to put their plan into action. With his heart pounding and his mind focused, Ethan locked eyes with Alexander, finding reassurance in the leader's unwavering gaze. They were ready to face whatever lay ahead, armed with the strength of their convictions and the power of unity. As the clash of wills and the intensity of the impending struggle hung in the air, Ethan felt a surge of determination. They would not be prisoners any longer. With the rebel army at their back and their shared resolve burning brightly, Ethan and his companions were ready to take their first steps toward freedom. Alexander's voice boomed with authority as he addressed the group, "Remember, we fight not only for ourselves but for all those who have suffered under the regime's iron fist. Today, we take the first step in reclaiming our future. Stay strong, stay focused, and let our actions speak louder than words." Ethan's heart swelled with a newfound sense of purpose. He knew that their path to freedom would be arduous, but the weight of responsibility only fueled his determination. His gaze shifted to the faces of his comrades, seeing the shared determination etched in their expressions. Together, they embodied the resilience and unyielding spirit of the rebel army. As the guards approached, Ethan steeled himself, adrenaline coursing through his veins. The moment of truth they had arrived. Captain Grace, leading by example, launched herself at the guards with a ferocity that ignited the flames of rebellion. The clash was swift and fierce, the rebel army coordinating their efforts flawlessly, overpowering their captors with calculated precision.

A wave of uncertainty and hope washed over the captives. Their eyes locked onto Ethan, searching for the spark of courage within themselves. Slowly, their fear transformed into determination, and with each passing moment, the group grew in numbers. The prisoners shed their shackles, both physical and metaphorical, joining the ranks of the rebel army as the rebellion gained momentum; the prison block became a battleground, the clash of steel and cries of defiance echoing through the corridors. The guards fought tooth and nail, desperate to maintain their grip on power. But against the united force of the rebel army, their resistance crumbled.

Ethan fought alongside his comrades, the weight of their shared purpose guiding every strike, every parry. The sense of camaraderie and solidarity fueled their resolve, empowering them to overcome every obstacle in their path. The rebel army proved themselves to be a force to be reckoned with, their spirits unbreakable. Finally, victory was within reach. The last remaining guards retreated, their defeat an undeniable testament to the strength of the rebellion. The prison block, once a symbol of oppression, had become a beacon of hope and defiance. As the echoes of the battle subsided, the rebel army took a moment to regroup, their collective breaths ragged but triumphant. Ethan turned to Alexander, his eyes filled with gratitude. "Thank you, Alexander. Your leadership and unwavering spirit have led us to this moment."

Alexander's gaze met Ethan's, pride and determination shining in his eyes. "We are all leaders in this fight, Ethan. Together, we will dismantle the corrupt regime and restore freedom to New Eden. Our journey has just begun." With those words, the rebel army prepared to press forward, their steps resonating with purpose.

CHAPTER TEN

Uncovering Secrets

Ethan and his group, battered and weary from their escape, trudged through the dense forest under the guidance of the rebel leader Alexander. Their steps were heavy, and the weight of their recent struggles clung to their every movement. Yet, a flicker of determination burned within each of them, propelling them forward through the rugged terrain. As they ventured deeper into the forest, the ambiance shifted. The sounds of civilization faded, replaced by the rustling of leaves and the distant calls of birds. The towering trees seemed to lean closer as if they were protectors guiding the way. And then, like a hidden gem tucked away in nature's embrace, the rebel camp came into view. Ethan's eyes widened, his breath catching in his throat. The camp was a testament to resilience and defiance—a vibrant sanctuary within the desolation of the world outside.

Tents of all shapes and sizes dotted the landscape, their colors blending harmoniously with the earthy tones of the forest. Makeshift buildings, crafted with resourcefulness and ingenuity, stood tall, offering refuge and a semblance of permanence. A symphony of voices filled the air, the camp buzzing with whispered conversations, laughter, and the clatter of daily life. Ethan's group was met with wary yet welcoming smiles as they entered the camp. Rebels of all ages and backgrounds moved with purpose, bound by the shared purpose that brought them together—the fight against the oppressive regime. Each face bore the marks of determination, etched by the hardships they had endured and the battles they had fought. Children played and laughed, their innocence a beacon of hope amidst the darkness. Elders imparted wisdom and shared stories of resistance, their eyes reflecting both the weight of their experiences and the enduring spirit within them. A sense of camaraderie and unity permeated the atmosphere as if the very air crackled with a shared purpose.

Ethan and his companions felt a warmth settle within their weary hearts, a sense of belonging and hope rekindled. They had found a community that dared to dream of a better world, a sanctuary that defied the regime's rule and nurtured the seeds of rebellion. As the sun dipped below the horizon, casting golden hues upon the camp, Ethan took a moment to breathe in the serenity and strength that surrounded him. In this hidden enclave amidst the wilderness, they were not alone. They were among those who believed, those who fought, and those who carried the torch of hope. The rebel camp pulsated with life, promising a future where justice would prevail and freedom would reign. Ethan's gaze met the determined eyes of his companions, a silent acknowledgment passing between them. They were ready to stand shoulder to shoulder with their newfound allies, united in purpose and fueled by the shared desire for a brighter tomorrow.

At the heart of the rebel camp, bathed in the warm glow of campfires, stood Jeremiah. His weathered face held the stories of a thousand battles, etched with lines that spoke of endurance and resilience. The light danced in his eyes, reflecting the flames that burned within his soul. Jeremiah, the oldest living man in the rebellion, had witnessed the rise and fall of civilizations. He had known the depths of despair and the heights of hope. His unwavering belief in a better future had driven him to ignite the flames of rebellion against the oppressive regime. As Ethan and his companions approached, Jeremiah beckoned them forward with a gnarled hand, his eyes shining with a mixture of wisdom and determination. They gathered around him, their anticipation palpable in the heavy air. The weight of the secrets about to be unveiled settled upon them like a cloak, each breath filled with a mixture of trepidation and resolve.

At that moment, time seemed to stand still. The crackling of the campfire, the rustle of leaves in the wind, and the murmurs of the rebel camp faded into the background. All that remained was the presence of Jeremiah, a beacon of hope amidst the chaos and despair that plagued their world. Ethan and his companions, their gazes fixed upon the aged rebel leader, hung on every word that fell from his lips. They sensed that this pivotal moment held the potential to change the course of their lives, to unravel the secrets that shrouded New Eden and paved the path towards a brighter future. With a voice that carried the weight of history, Jeremiah began to speak. His words wove a tapestry of revelation and truth, unveiling the darkness that had concealed the heart of their supposed utopia.

As Jeremiah spoke, his voice carried the weight of years of knowledge and the burden of the dark secrets hidden within the supposed utopia of New Eden. The revelations that unfolded painted a bleak and sinister picture, shattering the illusions that had been carefully crafted by the corrupt leaders. He began by exposing the exploitation that fueled the regime's power. New Eden, once thought to be a haven of prosperity, thrived on the backs of the suffering masses. The resources that sustained the city were acquired through ruthless means, stripping the land of its abundance while leaving the majority of its inhabitants impoverished and destitute. The stark contrast between the opulence of the ruling elite and the despair of the forgotten underclass was laid bare.

Jeremiah delved deeper, revealing the depths of corruption and oppression that tainted New Eden. The regime ruthlessly suppressed dissent, stifling any voice of opposition through coercion, propaganda, and fear. Free thought was crushed under the weight of censorship, leaving the citizens deprived of their right to question and challenge the status quo. Any semblance of individuality was suffocated in the name of maintaining control. But it was not only the physical and mental oppression that plagued

New Eden. The regime's insidious grasp extended into the very foundations of society, manipulating the lives of its citizens in ways they could scarcely imagine. Lives were manipulated, destinies were controlled, and choices were mere illusions. The inhabitants of New Eden were little more than pawns in a grand scheme designed to consolidate power and maintain the ruling elite's stranglehold on the city.

Jeremiah's words painted a picture of a society built on a foundation of lies and manipulation. Behind the shiny façade of prosperity, New Eden hid a dark underbelly, where the corrupt leaders reveled in their power and privilege, disregarding the suffering they caused to maintain their grip on authority. Ethan and his companions absorbed the weight of these revelations, their minds spinning with the implications of the dark secrets exposed. The utopia they had yearned for had crumbled, replaced by a profound sense of betrayal and outrage. The spark of rebellion within their hearts burned brighter as they realized that their fight was not merely for survival but for the liberation of all those ensnared in the web of New Eden's deceit.

Jeremiah's presence radiated strength, inspiring those around him to rise above their fears and embrace the cause that united them. At that moment, the rebel camp became more than just a gathering of individuals; it transformed into a community fueled by a shared purpose and an unyielding desire for change. With each passing revelation, Ethan felt the fire within him grow stronger. The weight of the secrets they carried had burdened his spirit, but now, in the presence of Jeremiah and the collective resolve of the rebels, that weight lifted, replaced by a sense of purpose and a thirst for justice. The crackling campfire illuminated the faces of those gathered, casting dancing shadows across their determined expressions. Jeremiah's voice carried the weight of wisdom and experience as he shared the stories of those who had fallen victim to the regime's oppression. Each tale ignited a spark within Ethan's heart, fueling his resolve to fight for a better future.

As the night wore on, time seemed to stand still. The air was charged with anticipation, with the shared understanding that they stood on the precipice of something greater. Jeremiah's words resonated, weaving through the hearts and minds of each present, kindling a flame that refused to be extinguished. Ethan exchanged glances with his companions, their eyes shining with a newfound determination. The paths that had brought them together had been filled with hardship and adversity, but in that moment, they felt a kinship that transcended their past struggles. They were part of something bigger—a rebellion that sought to reclaim their freedom and restore justice to their shattered society. Jeremiah's storytelling painted a vivid picture of the injustices they would face, but it also imbued them with a sense of purpose and camaraderie. They knew that the journey ahead would be arduous, filled with trials and sacrifices, but they were willing to face whatever came their way.

"And so, my friends," Jeremiah concluded, his voice resonating with unwavering resolve, "we stand at the precipice of change. We have the power to tear down the facade, to reclaim what has been stolen from us. Our rebellion grows stronger by the day, bolstered by the righteousness of our cause. Will you stand with us?" Ethan and his companions exchanged determined glances, their answers clear. They would stand united, shoulder to shoulder, to expose the dark secrets of New Eden and restore hope to a broken world. The rebellion had found its purpose, and the battle for justice had only just begun. Jeremiah's words lingered in the air, leaving a charge of anticipation and resolve. The camp around them hummed with renewed energy as rebels prepared themselves for the daunting path that lay ahead. Each member of the group understood the weight of their decision, the risks they would face, and the sacrifices they would make. But the glimmer of hope burned brightly in their hearts, fanning the flames of their determination.

With every passing moment, their bond grew stronger. They were no longer just individuals seeking their salvation; they were a collective force, bound together by a shared vision of a brighter future. The rebellion became a beacon of hope in a world shrouded in darkness and despair. As they prepared to face the challenges that lay ahead, Ethan couldn't help but feel a glimmer of hope, knowing that the rebellion's cause was just, and their determination unbreakable. They had witnessed the power of unity, the strength that could be found in the collective will of the oppressed. It was this spirit that would guide them through the darkest of times, propelling them forward with unwavering resolve. In the coming days, they would face danger, betrayal, and uncertainty. They would encounter hardships that would test their mettle and push them to their limits. But in their hearts, they carried the unwavering belief that justice would prevail. The secrets of New Eden would be exposed, the oppressive regime would crumble, and a new dawn would rise.

As they stood amid the rebel camp, Ethan and his companions felt the weight of responsibility upon their shoulders. They were the harbingers of change, the catalysts for a revolution that would shake the foundations of their broken world. They were ready to march forward, side by side, their spirits fueled by the fire of justice and the hope that their actions would pave the way for a better tomorrow. The rebellion had found its purpose, and as they embraced that purpose, they vowed to never falter. Their determination would carry them through the darkest of nights, guiding them toward a lost horizon where freedom and justice would reign. With hearts full of resolve, they embraced the challenges that awaited them, knowing that together, united in their cause, they were unstoppable. The stage was set, the battle lines drawn. The rebellion was poised to make its mark on history, and as the echoes of Jeremiah's words faded into the night.

CHAPTER ELEVEN

The Rebellion Takes Shape

As the flickering torches cast dancing shadows upon the walls of the dimly lit underground hideout, Ethan stood before the gathered rebels, his voice steady and his eyes filled with a burning determination. The weight of the regime's corruption bore down on their shoulders, fueling their collective desire for justice and freedom. Ethan's words rang out, cutting through the heavy air. His voice, filled with conviction, echoed through the underground chambers. He spoke of the necessity for a rebellion that was not only driven by passion but tempered by strategic planning and unwavering unity. Each word carried the weight of their shared purpose, igniting a fire within the hearts of the rebels. The atmosphere in the hideout shifted as the rebels listened intently, their spirits rising, their doubts replaced by a renewed sense of purpose. Ethan's impassioned words painted a vivid picture of the world they could build together, a world where hope thrived, where fairness reigned, and where the chains of oppression were shattered.

They understood that their fight was not merely against the regime itself, but against the very notion of their humanity being suppressed and controlled. Their cause transcended personal vendettas or grievances; it became a beacon of light in the darkness, a symbol of resistance against the forces that sought to strip them of their dignity. As Ethan continued to speak, his voice grew stronger, resonating with the hearts and minds of the rebels. He kindled their courage, reminding them that they were not alone and that they stood united against a common enemy. His words wove a tapestry of unity, threading together their diverse backgrounds, experiences, and aspirations into a single powerful force. At that moment, the dimly lit hideout transformed into a sanctuary of collective determination. The flickering torches seemed to burn brighter, casting long shadows that merged, symbolizing the merging of their hopes and dreams into a shared destiny. They knew that together they were unstoppable, their spirits bound together by an unbreakable bond.

As Ethan's speech drew to a close, the air buzzed with anticipation and resolve. The rebels exchanged glances, their eyes gleaming with a newfound sense of purpose. They were no longer a scattered group of individuals; they were a united front, ready to challenge the regime, ready to reclaim their city and their lives. In that dimly lit underground hideout, Ethan had not only addressed a gathering of rebels, but he had sparked a flame within each one of them. They left the hideout with their hearts aflame, ready to face the challenges that lay ahead, knowing that their fight was not in vain. The rebellion had taken shape, and its strength would be tested in the battles to come. With a shared vision and Ethan's unwavering leadership, they would march forward, steadfast in their pursuit of justice and freedom, knowing that they held the power to reshape their world and forge a brighter future. The dimly lit hideout had become a sanctuary of hope, and the rebels, fueled by Ethan's impassioned words, were ready to carry that hope into the world outside.

Ethan carefully selects individuals he trusts to hold key positions within the rebellion, recognizing the importance of their unique strengths and abilities. As he delegates responsibilities, he knows that the success of their cause relies on the collective efforts of a diverse group of individuals. One of the first allies appointed by Ethan is Liam Carter, a skilled strategist with a keen tactical mind. Liam's ability to analyze complex situations and devise effective plans makes him an invaluable asset in the rebellion's operations. His strategic thinking and calm demeanor inspire confidence in the other rebels. Another trusted ally is Olivia Ramirez, a talented medic with a deep sense of compassion. Olivia's healing abilities and extensive medical knowledge ensure that the rebels are well cared for in times of injury or illness. She works tirelessly to ensure their physical well-being, bringing hope and comfort to those who need it most.

To strengthen their defenses, Ethan turns to Marcus Davis, an expert in engineering and fortifications. Marcus's expertise in constructing defensive structures and devising traps proves instrumental in fortifying the rebellion's safe houses. With his guidance, the rebels gain an advantage by creating ingenious obstacles that catch the regime's forces off guard. Ethan also appoints Ava Patel as the intelligence officer of the rebellion. Ava's skills as a hacker and her vast network of contacts within the city's underbelly provide the rebels with vital information about the regime's movements and plans. Her ability to navigate the digital realm and gather valuable intelligence is crucial in staying one step ahead of their enemies. In addition to these key allies, Captain Grace Thompson mobilizes her band of survivors, each bringing their own invaluable experiences and resourcefulness to the cause. Among them is Sergeant Victor Chen, a seasoned soldier whose military training and discipline inspire the rebels and instill a sense of order within their ranks. Sarah, Ethan's younger sister, steps forward with unwavering determination and unwavering faith in their cause.

Ethan found a moment to speak privately with his younger sister, Sarah, amidst the bustling preparations for the upcoming battle. Concern etched his face as he gently grasped her arm, leading her to a quieter corner of their makeshift headquarters. "Sis, I need to talk to you," Ethan began, his voice filled with a mix of worry and determination. "This fight, it's going to be dangerous. More dangerous than anything we've faced before." Sarah looked up at her brother, her eyes reflecting a mix of determination and apprehension. "I know, Ethan. But I want to help. I want to fight alongside you." Ethan sighed, his brows furrowing with a mix of love and concern. "Sarah, you're so important to me. You're important to all of us. That's why I need you to stay back, to stay safe." Sarah's face fell, her voice wavering slightly. "But I can't just sit idly by while everyone else fights for what's right. I want to be a part of this, Ethan. I want to make a difference."

Ethan's grip on Sarah's arm tightened ever so slightly, conveying both his love and his protective instincts. "And you are making a difference, Sarah. Your strength and resilience inspire all of us. But your safety, your well-being, that's just as important. I can't bear the thought of something happening to you." Tears welled up in Sarah's eyes as she looked up at her brother, her voice barely above a whisper. "I understand your concern, Ethan, but I can't simply hide away while you and everyone else risk their lives. We're in this together." Ethan's gaze softened, his heart swelling with pride for his sister's bravery. He cupped her face gently in his hands. "Sarah, you've always been my inspiration. Your unwavering spirit is what keeps us going. But your role in this fight doesn't have to be on the front lines. We need you differently. We need your hope, your compassion, and your ability to inspire others. You'll be our beacon, our symbol of what we're fighting for."

Sarah's tears gave way to a mixture of understanding and determination. She nodded, her voice filled with newfound resolve. "Okay, Ethan. I'll stay back, but I promise you, I'll do everything I can to support our cause. I won't let you down." Ethan's expression softened, and he pulled Sarah into a tight embrace. "I know you won't, Sarah. You're stronger than you realize. We'll fight for a better future together, side by side, even if our roles are different." As they held each other, the weight of their shared purpose and love for one another infused them with renewed determination. They knew that their paths might diverge on the battlefield, but their bond would remain unbreakable. With the understanding reached between them, Ethan and Sarah rejoined the preparations, their commitment to the cause stronger than ever.

Ethan gathers his trusted allies in a dimly lit room, their eyes focused and determined. The time has come to plan their attack on the corrupt regime in New Eden. With a detailed map of the city spread out before them, Ethan points to strategic locations where they will strike, each one carefully chosen to maximize their chances of success. "Our first target," Ethan declares, pointing to a sprawling building in the heart of the city, "is the Citadel of Justice. This is where the regime's leaders reside, surrounded by their loyal guards. Taking control of the Citadel will deal a severe blow to their morale and disrupt their command structure." Ethan's finger then moves to a heavily fortified structure situated on the outskirts of the city. "The Central Supply Depot is vital for the regime's survival," he continues. "It's where they stockpile resources and weapons. By seizing this depot, we cripple their ability to sustain their forces and arm themselves." Next, Ethan directs their attention to a bustling marketplace, where the regime enforces its control over the citizens.

"The Market Square has become a symbol of the regime's oppression. We will liberate it and show the people that they no longer have to live in fear. This will inspire others to join our cause." Ethan's gaze shifts to a prominent broadcast tower that looms over the city. "The Propaganda Broadcast Center is responsible for disseminating the regime's lies and propaganda. By taking control of this tower, we will reclaim the narrative, spreading the truth and rallying more people to our cause." With each target identified, Ethan assigns specific teams of rebels to each location, taking into account their unique skills and abilities. Liam's strategic mind makes him the ideal leader for the assault on the Citadel of Justice, while Olivia's medical expertise is crucial in ensuring the wounded are cared for during the operation. Ava's intelligence-gathering skills are put to use in coordinating the attack on the Central Supply Depot, where her knowledge of the regime's supply routes and defenses will be invaluable. Marcus's engineering prowess is tapped to devise a plan to breach the Market Square's heavily guarded entrances, utilizing his knowledge to create diversions and exploit weaknesses.

Ethan set out to establish safe houses, hidden pockets of resistance within the decaying city. With the help of his allies, they scouted abandoned buildings and forgotten tunnels, carefully selecting locations away from prying eyes. Each safe house became a sanctuary, a place where rebels could find solace, train, and prepare for the battles to come. The safe houses buzzed with activity, vibrant hubs of resistance that pulsed with the energy of rebellion. Inside, the air crackled with determination as rebels of all ages and backgrounds gathered. The space transformed into a melting pot of stories, experiences, and shared purpose. In these makeshift training grounds, the rebels honed their skills. They taught each other survival techniques, combat strategies, and methods to outsmart the regime's forces. Maya, with her expertise in martial arts, led intense training sessions, pushing the rebels to their limits and unlocking hidden potential within them.

Amid the training, the safe houses became more than just spaces to practice physical skills. They fostered a sense of community and camaraderie. Rebels shared their personal stories, scars of the past that bound them together in their fight for freedom. They found solace in knowing they were not alone, finding support and strength in their shared struggle. Ethan understood that the rebellion needed more than just skilled fighters. They required resources to sustain their cause. With a determined glint in his eye, Ethan devised daring plans to raid the regime's warehouses and armories. Under the cover of darkness, the rebels infiltrated these heavily guarded locations, seizing weapons, ammunition, and supplies. Through these audacious raids, the rebels not only secured arms but also gathered vital intelligence. They unearthed information about the regime's supply routes, discovering weaknesses that could be exploited. By studying hidden caches and decoding encrypted communications, they gained valuable advantages for the upcoming battle.

Ethan's leadership shone during these perilous missions. He guided the rebels with precision and foresight, ensuring their safety and success. His strategic mind and ability to think on his feet made him a respected figure among the ranks, inspiring others to push beyond their limits. As the safe houses grew in number and the rebellion expanded, Ethan's vision began to take shape. The safe houses became vital hubs, thriving with activity and filled with hope. Rebels, once scattered and isolated, now stood united, connected by a common purpose and the unbreakable bonds forged through shared hardship.

Ethan stood before the gathered rebels, his eyes reflecting the flickering light of a nearby candle. His voice, filled with a mix of determination and vulnerability, resonated through the room. The rebels hushed, eagerly awaiting his words. "My friends, comrades, and fellow rebels," Ethan began, his voice steady but laced with emotion. "Today, we stand on the precipice of change. The path we have chosen is not an easy one, but it is one worth fighting for." He paused, taking a deep breath, gathering his thoughts. Memories of his father flooded his mind, the longing for his presence intensifying with each passing day. Ethan's voice trembled slightly as he continued, "I stand before you today not only as a leader but as someone who understands the weight of our struggle. Like many of you, I have lost loved ones to the chaos and devastation that engulfs our world. I miss my father every day, and the hope of finding him within the walls of New Eden has driven me forward."

Ethan locked eyes with those before him, his gaze unwavering. "But this fight, my friends, is not just about finding our loved ones. It is about reclaiming our humanity, about giving voice to the voiceless, and about forging a future where every person, every child, has the chance to live free from oppression." His voice grew stronger, a passion infusing every word. "In this room, we are not just rebels. We are the embodiment of resilience, the living proof that hope can thrive even in the darkest of times. We have experienced loss, we have felt fear, but it is through our shared struggle that we have found strength. We are united by the belief that a better world is possible." Ethan's eyes scanned the room, capturing the faces of those who had joined him on this perilous journey. "Today, we are not alone. Today, we stand together as a force to be reckoned with. Our hearts beat as one, pulsing with the desire for justice, for freedom. Let our actions speak louder than the words of the regime. Let our unwavering resolve shake the foundations of their corrupt rule."

He extended a hand, a gesture of solidarity. "I ask every one of you to commit to this cause, to fight with unwavering dedication, and to support each other in the face of adversity. Together, we will tear down the walls that imprison us. Together, we will build a future that generations to come will be proud to inherit." Ethan's voice rang out, infused with hope and determination. "Our journey to New Eden is not just about finding salvation for ourselves. It is about bringing salvation to all of humanity. Let us march forward, my friends, with courage in our hearts and the knowledge that we are on the right side of history." As the echoes of Ethan's words settled in the room, a resounding roar of agreement and determination rose from the rebels. They stood taller, their resolve steeled, ready to face the battles ahead. Inspired by Ethan's emotional speech, they were united in their mission—to tear down the regime, find their loved ones, and build a future worthy of their dreams.

CHAPTER TWELVE

Infiltrating the Palace

As night draped its comforting shroud over the decaying city, Ethan and his team gathered in a hidden safe house nestled amidst the abandoned ruins. The flickering candlelight cast dancing shadows on their determined faces, setting the stage for their audacious plan. In their possession were stolen blueprints, a treasure trove of crucial information that would pave the way for their infiltration of the opulent palace—the symbol of the regime's power and corruption. The stolen blueprints had been acquired through a perilous web of underground contacts and carefully executed reconnaissance missions. Ethan had tirelessly cultivated relationships with those who resented the regime's tyrannical rule, skillfully coaxing information from the hearts of disillusioned insiders.

One moonless night, beneath the cover of darkness, Ethan skillfully evaded patrolling guards and deactivated state-of-the-art security systems. Their nimble movements guided them through labyrinthine hallways, leading them ever closer to the heart of the regime's stronghold. With the grace of a seasoned thief, Ethan bypassed intricate locks and accessed the official's office, his heart pounding in anticipation of the valuable information that lay within. He quickly scanned the room, his eyes catching the glimmer of hope—a secured cabinet, rumored to house classified blueprints of the palace. Time was of the essence as Ethan skillfully picked the lock and retrieved the cabinet's contents. He meticulously photographed the intricate blueprints, ensuring that no detail would escape their grasp. The blueprints were the key to their success, laying bare the vulnerabilities and hidden passages that would guide them past the fortress's formidable defenses.

Their audacity did not stop at the stolen blueprints alone. Over weeks and months, Ethan and his team operated like a clandestine network, their eyes and ears attuned to every opportunity. They gathered vital intelligence from disillusioned palace servants, desperate for a chance to see the regime's reign crumble. Their sources within the palace walls were risky yet invaluable. A disgruntled servant, burdened with the weight of loyalty to the regime, had shared snippets of conversations overheard between corrupt leaders. A guard, swayed by the rebels' promise of a better future, provided insight into the ever-changing rotations and vulnerabilities in the palace's security.

Ethan methodically pieced together each fragment of information, cross-referencing it against the stolen blueprints. Their preparations were meticulous, their minds racing with the multitude of challenges they would face within the opulent palace's fortified walls. Late nights were spent analyzing every detail, pouring over the blueprints to understand the palace's inner workings. Ethan traced his finger along the intricate maze of corridors, hidden chambers, and guarded entrances, committing each twist and turn to memory. He knew that every decision, every step, had to be executed flawlessly to avoid capture or the fate that awaited those who opposed the regime. Countless hours were devoted to honing their skills, conducting simulated missions, and perfecting their ability to move with the silence and precision of ghosts. They practiced disabling security systems, evading patrolling guards, and executing swift takedowns. The team's unwavering dedication and resilience transformed them into a formidable force, ready to face the regime's elite defenders.

As the night sky witnessed their tireless efforts, Ethan and his team finalized their plans, their resolve steeling against the challenges that awaited them. Armed with stolen blueprints and the priceless knowledge procured through daring acts of infiltration, they stood poised to infiltrate the impenetrable palace—the epicenter of the regime's power. In the dimly lit safe house, bathed in the flickering glow of the candle, Ethan's gaze lingered on the stolen blueprints spread before him. Their value was immeasurable, their presence a testament to the determination and sacrifice of those who had contributed to the rebellion's cause.

Ethan and his team, their faces etched with determination, gathered within the hidden safe house. The dim light cast flickering shadows across the room as they huddled around a weathered table, strewn with stolen blueprints and marked with red and black lines. The plans before them revealed the inner workings of the opulent palace, the heart of the regime's power. With a furrowed brow, Ethan studied the intricate maze of corridors, hidden chambers, and guarded entrances that made up the palace. His finger traced the convoluted paths, mapping them into his mind with meticulous precision. Every twist and turn, every secret passage and concealed doorway, he committed to memory. Each member of the team did the same, absorbing the layout, and understanding that knowledge of the palace's inner workings was crucial for their mission. The stolen blueprints, acquired through risky espionage, offered a glimpse into the inner sanctum of the regime's stronghold. They depicted the palace's sprawling halls, ornate chambers, and heavily fortified sections. It was a fortress, a symbol of the regime's power and corruption. Infiltrating it would be their greatest challenge yet.

As dusk descended upon the city, shrouding it in an inky veil, the team donned their black attire, blending into the shadows cast by the crumbling buildings and forgotten alleyways. Their movements were deliberate and silent, like phantoms navigating through the decaying cityscape. They possessed stealth honed through countless missions, each step calculated to avoid detection. Their hearts beat in unison, a steady rhythm echoing the anticipation that filled the air. Each member of the team understood the risks they were undertaking, and the consequences of failure. The fate of the rebellion rested on their shoulders, and the weight of that responsibility was both daunting and invigorating. They maneuvered through the city, their senses heightened, their awareness acute. Their progress was a dance of agility and caution, avoiding patrols and surveillance, slipping past sentries stationed at strategic points. They utilized their knowledge of the city's hidden pathways, ducking through narrow passages, scaling crumbling walls, and vanishing into the darkness whenever danger lurked nearby.

The team moved like shadows, weaving through the labyrinthine streets, guided by the stolen blueprints imprinted in their minds. Their collective focus never wavered as they navigated the treacherous terrain. Each step forward brought them closer to their target, the opulent palace gleaming in the distance, its grandeur contrasting with the desolation that surrounded it. As they neared their objective, the air crackled with a blend of tension and excitement. The palace, a fortress of marble and gilded opulence, loomed before them, its towering walls a testament to the regime's power. Towering guards stood at attention, their eyes watchful, ready to defend the regime's stronghold at any cost. Ethan's team blended into the shadows, hiding in alcoves and behind crumbling pillars. They observed the guards, studying their patterns, seeking the right moment to strike. Their mission demanded flawless execution, and any misstep could spell disaster. Their hearts pounded in their chests as they prepared to make their move. The team shared one last glance, a silent affirmation of their commitment to the cause. With a nod from Ethan, they unleashed their well-practiced skills, coordinating their actions with precision.

Swiftly and silently, the team neutralized the guards, their movements honed from countless hours of training. Disabling their opponents without a sound, they hid the unconscious bodies, ensuring their infiltration remained undetected. As the team regrouped, they took a moment to breathe, their eyes fixed on the grand entrance of the palace. Ahead lay the epicenter of the regime's power, their objective within reach. Their hearts raced with a mix of trepidation and determination. They knew that the true test of their skills and resilience was about to begin—a battle not only against physical obstacles but also against the darkness that had gripped their city for far too long.

Finally, after traversing a labyrinth of ornate corridors and bypassing multiple layers of security, Ethan and his team found themselves standing before the heavily guarded doors of the opulent chamber. The doors, adorned with intricate carvings and gilded handles, seemed to mock the rebels, a symbol of the impenetrable fortress they were about to breach. With cautious determination, Ethan signaled his team to proceed. They worked in perfect synchrony, using their acquired knowledge and carefully crafted tools to deactivate security systems and slip past the watchful eyes of the guards. Each step brought them closer to the heart of the palace, where the corrupt leaders resided. As they entered the chamber, the air grew thick with an unsettling aura. The room dripped with opulence, adorned with lavish tapestries, crystal chandeliers, and towering statues. The trappings of power surrounded the corrupt leaders, who sat behind grand desks, engrossed in their schemes and oblivious to the impending threat.

Ethan's heart pounded in his chest as he stepped forward, his eyes burning with a fire fueled by years of oppression and longing for justice. The leaders looked up, their faces etched with shock and disbelief as they registered the presence of the rebels. The confrontation they had never anticipated had arrived. Silence enveloped the room as Ethan's voice pierced through the air, strong and resolute. He spoke with a blend of anger, determination, and compassion, delivering the rebellion's message with unwavering conviction. The weight of their malevolence hung heavily, but Ethan's words reverberated, piercing through the walls they had erected to shield themselves from the suffering of the people they had exploited. A tense standoff ensued as the leaders, their arrogance momentarily shattered, grappled with the realization that their reign was crumbling. Fear and desperation flickered across their faces, mirroring the anguish of the countless lives they had oppressed for far too long. The rebellion had materialized before their eyes, a force of united defiance that they could no longer dismiss or ignore.

Ethan's team, united in purpose and fueled by their shared struggle, stood behind him, an unwavering wall of determination. They outnumbered and outmatched the leaders, their weapons glinting in the dim light. The rebels were a living testament to the power of unity and the indomitable spirit of those who yearned for freedom. The room crackled with tension, each passing moment heightening the stakes. The leaders, cornered and stripped of their illusions of invincibility, scrambled for a response. But their feeble attempts to retain control were no match for the strength of the rebellion, fortified by the resilience and unyielding spirit of the people they had long suppressed. In that pivotal moment, the rebellion's uprising became tangible. The air crackled with anticipation as if the very walls of the chamber were trembling with the weight of change. It was a turning point—an indelible mark in history where the oppressive regime began its descent into oblivion. And so, the standoff continued, the leaders confronted by a force they could not overcome. The regime's grip on power crumbled as the rebellion's message reverberated through the room, resounding with the hope of a future where justice would prevail. Ethan and his team stood as beacons of light amidst the darkness, embodying the dreams and aspirations of an entire city. The oppressive reign was coming to an end, and the regime's fear now mirrored the desperation of those they had oppressed.

As the tense standoff in the opulent chamber reached its zenith, a chilling realization spread among Ethan and his team. The room, once a symbol of the regime's power, now revealed itself as nothing more than a deceptive façade—a carefully crafted illusion designed to divert attention from the truth. Amid their shock and confusion, it became evident that the leaders they had confronted had vanished, leaving behind only empty seats and a bitter taste of betrayal. The gravity of the situation weighed heavily upon Ethan and his team as they realized they had fallen victim to a meticulously orchestrated hoax. Eyes scanned the room in search of answers, landing on the vacant spot where Dr. Samuel Collins had been seated moments before. The brilliant scientist, once a trusted ally, had played a treacherous role in the deception. Ethan's heart sank as he realized that the man he had looked to for guidance and knowledge had been a puppet of the regime all along.

Feelings of anger and betrayal surged through the rebels, fueling their determination to uncover the truth and hold the traitor accountable. Questions flooded their minds, the most pressing being: What other deceptions had been carefully woven into their journey to New Eden? And where had the corrupt leaders truly fled? Ethan's resolve hardened in the face of this revelation. The rebellion, now stronger than ever, refused to succumb to despair. The escape of the leaders and the betrayal of Dr. Collins would not break their spirit or their determination to dismantle the regime. If anything, it ignited an even fiercer flame within their hearts—a flame fueled by justice, resilience, and a hunger for the truth.

With renewed purpose, Ethan turned to his team, meeting their eyes with steely resolve. He vowed that they would uncover the secrets shrouding New Eden, expose the regime's lies, and bring about the justice they had fought so hard to achieve. The escape of the leaders and the betrayal by Dr. Collins had only served to strengthen their resolve, pushing them further down the path of resistance. As they regrouped, Ethan made a solemn vow to his fellow rebels. The rebellion had taken another step forward, armed with the knowledge that only through the relentless pursuit of the truth could they reclaim their city and forge a future free from oppression.

CHAPTER THIRTEEN

The Chamber of Cryosleep

Exhausted but determined, Ethan and his allies make their way back from the battlefield to the safe house. The streets are eerily quiet, bearing the scars of the recent clash between the rebels and the regime's forces. As they cautiously navigate the rubble-strewn path, Ethan's keen intuition guides him toward an unusual shimmer of light emanating from a partially collapsed building. Curiosity piqued, Ethan veers off the main route and follows the elusive glow. The group cautiously enters the dilapidated structure, their steps echoing through the desolate corridors. The air is thick with dust and the remnants of forgotten memories. Suddenly, they stumble upon a hidden door, concealed behind a fallen bookcase. Ethan's pulse quickens, sensing that there is something significant beyond that barrier. With a collective effort, they push aside the debris, revealing a hidden passage leading to an underground chamber.

As they step into the chamber, a soft, ambient light fills the space, casting an otherworldly glow. Rows of cryosleep pods line the walls, resembling a haunting symphony of suspended animation. The room is cold, the air heavy with a sense of anticipation. Ethan's heart races with a mixture of hope and trepidation as he scans the pods, his eyes scanning each face in the delicate embrace of cryosleep. And then, his breath catches in his throat. There, nestled among the sleepers, is his father, Thomas Turner. Ethan moves closer, drawn to the sight of his father's peaceful visage, preserved in time. The pod is made of translucent material, revealing the intricate network of tubes and wires that sustain the sleeper's life force. A soft, rhythmic hum permeates the air, emanating from the control panel nearby.

Tears well up in Ethan's eyes as he reaches out to touch the surface of the pod, his fingers tingling with a mixture of disbelief and overwhelming joy. His father's presence, albeit suspended, brings a renewed sense of purpose and determination to his heart. Ethan's allies gather around him, sharing in the profound moment of reunion. They gaze in awe at the cryosleep chamber, their eyes flickering with a mix of awe and wonder. Ethan's heart races with anticipation as he and the rebels gather around the control panel of the cryosleep chamber. The panel is adorned with a series of intricate symbols and codes, its purpose shrouded in mystery. They understand that uncovering the truth behind these symbols could reveal not only the fate of the sleepers but also the secrets of New Eden itself. Grace, a seasoned military leader among the rebels, steps forward. Her eyes narrow as she studies the symbols, drawing upon her experience with advanced technology and military operations. She recognizes certain patterns, indicating a complex code that must be deciphered.

With a firm resolve, Grace begins to analyze the symbols, tracing the connections between different parts of the control panel. She notes that some of the symbols resemble military insignias she encountered during her time in the armed forces. This realization fuels her determination to solve the mystery and exposes a connection between the military and the creation of New Eden. As Grace delves deeper into the symbols and codes, she notices recurring motifs and a pattern hidden within the intricate design. She instinctively understands that these symbols hold a hidden message, a key to unlocking the truth. The rebels huddle around Grace, providing support and offering their insights as they collectively try to solve the mystery. They meticulously decipher the cryptic symbols, analyzing their placement and the patterns they form. Each revelation brings them closer to uncovering the secrets that lie within the control panel.

The control panel is a marvel of advanced technology, adorned with a myriad of symbols and cryptic codes. Grace examines the intricate engravings, noting the precision in their placement and the patterns they form. The symbols are unlike anything she has encountered before, suggesting that this technology far surpasses anything known in their dystopian world. Amidst the symbols, Grace identifies recurring patterns resembling a stylized phoenix—the mythical bird of rebirth and resurrection. The phoenix serves as a symbol of hope, and Grace wonders if this motif is indicative of New Eden's purpose—a sanctuary for humanity's rebirth. Grace and the rebels gather around the control panel, their heads together, as they try to decipher the coded messages. One of the symbols resembles a combination of ancient hieroglyphs and binary code. It seems to represent an encrypted message, and the rebels realize that solving it could unveil the secrets hidden within.

They carefully examine each symbol, assigning numbers and letters to their unique shapes. Grace uses her knowledge of military encryption techniques to identify patterns and potential key sequences. Slowly, she unravels the first layer of the coded message. One by one, the symbols reveal their hidden meanings. The coded message speaks of a "Project Phoenix," detailing plans to build an underground sanctuary to ensure humanity's survival. It outlines a comprehensive blueprint for reconstructing society after a cataclysmic event. Further decoding reveals information about the cryosleep chambers themselves—the technology behind them, the selection process for the sleepers, and the design of New Eden. Grace realizes that the military played a significant role in both constructing and overseeing the project.

As the rebels continue to decipher the codes, they find references to the "Council of Phoenix," a group of individuals who oversaw the construction of New Eden. However, the identity and whereabouts of these council members remain shrouded in mystery. Grace notices that a particular set of symbols appears repeatedly throughout the control panel. After careful examination, she realizes that these symbols form a sort of map—an intricate blueprint of New Eden's underground structure. Using the map, Grace identifies hidden compartments, secret passages, and concealed entrances within the facility. The map leads them to a previously unnoticed access panel in the control room. Excitement builds among the rebels as they believe it could hold the key to the cryosleep chambers' location.

With careful precision, Grace activates the access panel, revealing a holographic display that showcases the cryosleep chambers' layout. The sleepers' pods are organized in a grid-like formation, each connected to the central control system. Grace deciphers a final set of symbols on the holographic display, uncovering a hidden sequence that unlocks the cryosleep chambers. A soft hum fills the room as the pods begin to stir, and the sleepers' vital signs slowly rise. Their determination bearing fruit, the rebels rejoice in the success of their discovery. They understand that New Eden is not merely a utopia but a safeguard against humanity's extinction—a sanctuary for a brighter future. But as the holographic display flickers, a hidden message appears, indicating that New Eden was designed as a refuge from a global cataclysm—an event now ominously imminent. This revelation leaves the rebels with an even greater sense of urgency, knowing that time is running out to prevent the catastrophe and free the sleepers from their cryosleep chambers.

Through their collective efforts, they decipher a sequence of symbols that lead to a hidden compartment within the control panel. Inside, they find a dusty journal filled with faded ink and delicate sketches. The journal belongs to a scientist who was part of the team responsible for the development of the cryosleep chambers and New Eden. The entries in the journal reveal a startling truth. New Eden was not only created to preserve humanity but also to ensure its survival in the face of an impending global catastrophe. The military, recognizing the imminent collapse of society, had taken charge of the project, working in secret to establish a sanctuary where selected individuals would be preserved until the world could be rebuilt. The symbols and codes within the control panel were designed to safeguard the knowledge and technology necessary to rebuild society. Grace and the rebels piece together the fragments of information, connecting the dots and realizing the true scope of New Eden's purpose.

As the rebels continue their exploration of the holographic display, their attention is drawn to a peculiar symbol on the control panel—one that seems strangely familiar to Ethan. It resembles a delicate chain, similar to the one he wears around his neck, a cherished memento of his father. Ethan's heart quickens with hope as he examines the chain more closely. Grace, noticing the urgency in his eyes, encourages him to try placing the chain in a corresponding slot on the control panel. With trembling hands, Ethan follows her suggestion, and to his astonishment, the chain fits perfectly. As if responding to the connection, the holographic display shifts, revealing a series of symbols and coordinates. Grace realizes that the chain serves as a personalized key—a link between Ethan and his father's cryo-chamber. The chain contains encoded information specific to his family, a secret safeguarded for their reunion.

The coordinates lead to a specific chamber within the cryosleep facility. With determination and a mix of fear and excitement, Ethan, Captain Grace, and the other rebels set out to find the chamber that houses his father. As they approach the designated chamber, Ethan's heart pounds in anticipation. He places the chain into a slot beside the chamber's entrance, holding his breath as the cryo-chamber's door slowly slides open. A pale blue light emanates from within, casting an otherworldly glow over the room. And there, suspended in cryosleep, lies Ethan's father—resembling the father he once knew, preserved in a state of peaceful slumber. Ethan's eyes fill with tears of joy and relief as he steps forward to embrace his long-lost parent.

Grace and the other rebels stand by, allowing Ethan and his father a moment of private reunion. It is a bittersweet and emotional reunion, the weight of their time apart washed away by the sheer happiness of their togetherness once more. As Ethan's father begins to awaken, the room is filled with a soft, pulsating hum. The cryo-chamber releases its hold, gradually bringing him back to consciousness. As he opens his eyes, Ethan sees a mixture of confusion and recognition in his father's gaze.

"Ethan?" his father whispers, his voice trembling with disbelief.

"Dad, it's me. I found you," Ethan replies, his voice choked with emotion.

The two embrace, their bond stronger than ever before. Ethan's father expresses gratitude to the rebels for their rescue and gratitude to Ethan for finding him. Together, they share stories of their separate journeys—the struggles, the losses, and the hope that kept them going. With his father by his side, Ethan feels a newfound sense of purpose. They both understand that their reunion holds greater significance than just a personal connection—it symbolizes the hope of reuniting families torn apart by the regime and the promise of rebuilding a fractured society. As the rebels regroup, Ethan's father, now fully aware of the impending catastrophe, pledges to aid them in their fight against the regime. He brings valuable knowledge from his time within the cryosleep facility, giving the rebels a strategic advantage in their quest for justice.

CHAPTER FOURTEEN

Past

The safe house is enveloped in an air of weariness and relief as the rebels find a moment of respite from their constant struggle against the regime. They gather around, seeking solace and companionship amidst the turmoil that surrounds them. Ethan's father, Thomas Turner, observes their fatigue and realizes that the time has come to unburden his heart and share the untold history of New Eden. Thomas had carried the weight of this secret for too long, and he knew that revealing the truth was essential to strengthening the bonds among the rebels. He had seen how his son, Ethan, had matured through their journey, transforming from a street-smart teenager into a resilient leader, and he felt that Ethan was now ready to hear the truth.

One evening, after they have shared a simple meal, Thomas finds himself lost in thoughts of the past. He gazes at a family portrait that had survived the chaos of their world, and the memories come rushing back. The faces of loved ones who were lost, the sacrifices made for survival, and the vision that once brought hope for a brighter future—they all haunt him, demanding to be told. With a deep breath, Thomas stands before the gathered rebels, his heart heavy yet determined. His voice trembles slightly as he begins to speak, "I must share something with all of you—a truth that I've held close for far too long. It's about the origins of New Eden and how it was once conceived as a sanctuary for humanity's wellness."

Ethan and the others listen intently, their eyes fixed on Thomas, sensing the gravity of his words. He continues, "New Eden was more than just a utopian vision—it was an idea that emerged from the ashes of a collapsing society. Dr. Samuel Collins, a brilliant scientist, led the project, seeking to create a place of hope and healing for humanity."In the dimly lit safe house, Ethan's father, Thomas Foster, gathers the rebels around him, the soft glow of a lantern casting shadows on his face. He begins his tale with a distant look in his eyes as if he's transported back to a time long gone. "Before the chaos enveloped our world," Thomas starts, "there was a glimmer of hope—a vision to rebuild and create a new beginning for humanity. It was during a critical time when the remnants of our once-thriving society sought a path forward amidst the ruins."

Thomas explains that during those dark days, a group of exceptional individuals came together in a secret gathering known as the Round Table Conference. It was a gathering of brilliant minds—scientists, engineers, visionaries, and leaders from various fields—each with their unique expertise and a shared dream to forge a better future. At the center of this assemblage was Dr. Samuel Collins, a man of profound intellect and charisma. He was revered for his breakthroughs in advanced technology and his unwavering belief in the resilience of humanity. Dr. Collins spoke passionately about a utopian sanctuary called New Eden—a place where humanity could heal, rebuild, and thrive once more.

[Flashback Scene - Round Table Conference]

The conference room was bathed in soft light, and the air was thick with anticipation as the members of the Round Table Conference settled into their seats. At the head of the table, Dr. Samuel Collins, a visionary with a commanding presence, began the discussion.

Dr. Collins: (with a warm smile) "Thank you all for gathering here today. This conference marks the beginning of something extraordinary—a chance to reshape our world in the face of adversity. As we look around, we see a world crumbling, ravaged by conflict and devastation. But within each of us, there lies hope—a hope to rebuild and create a haven for humanity to thrive once more."

Evelyn Reynolds, a brilliant engineer, spoke up, her eyes gleaming with enthusiasm.

Evelyn: "Dr. Collins, your idea of a sanctuary, a place of healing and renewal, resonates deeply with all of us. It's a chance to unite our knowledge and expertise, to build something greater than ourselves. But how do we envision this sanctuary? What do we call it?"

Dr. Collins: (pausing for a moment, a touch of sadness crossing his face) "I have thought long and hard about this. I'd like to name it 'New Eden,' after my late wife, Eden. She was a woman of boundless compassion and love, and I can think of no better way to honor her memory than by creating a sanctuary where humanity can find solace and hope."

The room fell into contemplative silence, the weight of the name 'New Eden' settling upon them. Thomas Foster, Ethan's father, and an esteemed biologist, spoke with a sense of purpose.

Thomas: "Dr. Collins, your vision is powerful, and the name holds great significance. New Eden shall represent not just a sanctuary, but a symbol of hope—hope for a brighter future, where the mistakes of the past are learned from and never repeated."

Natalie Zhang, a charismatic leader known for her diplomacy, nodded in agreement.

Natalie: "Indeed, it's more than a refuge from the chaos. New Eden must become a community, a place where people come together, forging connections, and rebuilding not just buildings but the very fabric of society."

As the discussion continued, each member of the Round Table Conference added their unique insights, contributing to the vision of New Eden. Their shared dream of a sanctuary for humanity was born that day—a dream that would face trials and betrayals but would endure as a beacon of hope in the face of darkness.

Sebastian Ramirez, a seasoned historian with a keen understanding of society's rise and fall, raised a pertinent question.

Sebastian: "Dr. Collins, while we intend to create a haven, we must also address the potential for misuse of power. How do we ensure that New Eden remains true to its purpose and doesn't fall into the wrong hands?"

Dr. Collins: (nodding in agreement) "You raise a valid concern, Sebastian. We must establish principles that govern New Eden, ensuring transparency and accountability. It shall be a community governed by democracy and upheld by the people, so no individual can wield unchecked authority."

Evelyn: "I propose that we design a fail-safe system, limiting access to the most advanced technology and knowledge within New Eden. This way, we ensure that its potential for misuse is minimized."

Natalie: "Additionally, we must prioritize education and open discourse. By empowering the residents with knowledge and encouraging open dialogue, we foster a culture of informed decision-making and active participation."

As the ideas flowed freely, the Round Table Conference became a melting pot of ideals and possibilities. Thomas raised another concern, his brow furrowed with thoughtful consideration.

Thomas: "What about the selection process for those who seek refuge in New Eden? How do we ensure that the right people find solace within its walls?"

Dr. Collins: (with a compassionate smile) "We shall prioritize the value of life and compassion. New Eden shall open its doors to those who seek a chance at redemption and renewal. We shall strive to heal not just physical wounds but the scars of the heart and soul."

The conference room buzzed with hope and determination, the members united in their commitment to New Eden's vision. Thomas gazed around the table, his eyes shining with pride.

Thomas: "Today marks the beginning of our journey—a journey to build a sanctuary for humanity, a testament to the strength of hope and love in the face of despair."

The Round Table Conference concluded with an air of purpose and unity. As the members dispersed, they carried the weight of responsibility and the shared dream of a sanctuary that would endure through the ages.

[End of Flashback Scene]

One of the rebel members interrupts, "But how did someone like Dr. Collins turn to darkness and betray that noble vision?"

Thomas sighs, his expression clouded with sadness and regret. "That, my friends, is a tale of human frailty and ambition. As the construction of New Eden progressed, the pressures of rebuilding a shattered world took its toll on all of us. Dr. Collins, in particular, was burdened with an insatiable thirst for control and power. He became obsessed with the potential of New Eden's technology, envisioning it as a means to dominate rather than heal." Another rebel chimes in, "But didn't anyone see through his facade?"

Thomas nods, "Some did, but Dr. Collins was cunning. He gathered like-minded individuals around him, forming a hidden faction within the Round Table Conference. They presented a facade of unity, but their intentions were far darker than the vision we all shared. They manipulated and deceived us, masking their true ambitions while consolidating their grip on New Eden." The rebels listen intently, realizing the complexity of the situation they find themselves in. Thomas continues, "Eventually, it became evident that Dr. Collins and his faction had ulterior motives for New Eden. They wanted to wield its advanced technology to control and manipulate people, to enforce their rule upon those seeking refuge." "And the confrontation that followed?" another rebel asks.

"The confrontation was fierce," Thomas replies, his voice tinged with the pain of reliving those moments. "Those of us who were loyal to the original vision fought to preserve the sanctuary's true purpose. There was a battle of ideals and principles, a clash between hope and despair. In the end, Dr. Collins and his followers were banished, and the sanctuary was safeguarded, but the scars of betrayal remained." As the gravity of Thomas' words sinks in, Ethan feels a mixture of anger and determination building within him. He knows that to honor his father's sacrifices and the true vision of New Eden, they must confront the remnants of Dr. Collins' faction and ensure that darkness doesn't taint their dreams of a better world. As the rebels prepare for their next move, Thomas takes a deep breath, his voice steadying. "Now, we must uncover the remaining members of Dr. Collins' faction, to cleanse New Eden of its tainted past, and to rebuild the sanctuary as it was meant to be—a beacon of hope, healing, and rebirth for all of humanity."

CHAPTER FIFTEEN

The Hidden Chamber

Under the moonless sky, the rebels blend into the shadows, their faces smudged with dirt to better conceal themselves. Grace's eyes scan the imposing facade of the palace, its grandeur a stark reminder of the wealth amassed by the corrupt leaders at the expense of the suffering populace. She knows that their mission is fraught with danger, but the importance of uncovering the truth drives her forward. In hushed tones, Grace gathers the team around her, their breaths visible in the chilly night air. She lays out the plan, their every movement calculated to minimize risks and maximize their chances of success. "Thomas, Evelyn, and Natalie, you will create a diversion at the front gates," Grace says, her voice firm but tinged with an air of caution. "Ethan and I will head to the eastern wing to disable the surveillance systems and open a secret passage to the hidden chamber."

The team nods in understanding, their expressions are resolute despite the weight of their mission. They know that the fate of New Eden, the lives trapped in cryosleep, and the future of humanity hangs in the balance. Ethan grips the hilt of his makeshift weapon, a mixture of fear and determination swirling within him. His father's presence, standing by his side, provides both strength and reassurance. Thomas places a reassuring hand on his son's shoulder, wordlessly conveying his support and pride. As the groups disperse, Ethan and Grace navigate the treacherous grounds, avoiding the watchful gaze of guards patrolling the palace walls. The rebels' knowledge of the palace's layout, gained through stolen blueprints and careful observation, proves invaluable as they deftly steer clear of potential traps.

With each step, Ethan's heart races in tandem with the adrenaline coursing through his veins. He recalls the days spent honing his survival skills in the desolate wasteland of Earth, preparing for this very moment. He trusts in his training and the unity of their team. As they approach the eastern wing, Ethan and Grace come across a hidden panel concealed beneath an intricately carved column. Grace's nimble fingers work swiftly, entering a sequence of codes to deactivate the surveillance system guarding the corridor. Silence envelops them as they slip past the dormant surveillance drones. Ethan feels the weight of the responsibility on his shoulders, knowing that the success of their mission hinges on their ability to maintain stealth.

Thomas, his steady hands a product of both his expertise and years of survival on the city's unforgiving streets, surveys the palace's layout. His keen eye for detail, honed by his background in biology, proves invaluable. With whispered instructions, he guides the rebels through hidden corridors, avoiding surveillance cameras and laser sensors that would trigger alarms. As they navigate the labyrinthine palace, Evelyn's fingers dance across a portable hacking device. Her proficiency as an engineer becomes evident as she infiltrates the security system, momentarily gaining control over the surveillance feeds. Monitors display guards patrolling various sectors of the palace, their movements tracked by the rebels in real time. This access grants them a precious advantage, a fleeting glimpse into the regime's inner workings.

In a tense moment of high stakes, the rebels find themselves face-to-face with a detachment of elite guards, clad in imposing armor and armed with state-of-the-art weaponry. Their presence is a testament to the regime's paranoia and their resolve to protect the palace's secrets at all costs. It is then that Natalie steps forward, her posture radiating confidence and charm. Her skills as a diplomat, forged through years of negotiating with factions within the city, come to the forefront. As she engages the guards in conversation, her words are laced with a honeyed blend of flattery and intrigue, woven together in a delicate dance of deception.

The guards, momentarily captivated by Natalie's charisma, lower their guard. They are drawn into a world of words where uncertainty and suspicion are replaced with camaraderie. The conversation becomes a diversion—a cover for Ethan and the others to slip past undetected. With practiced coordination, the rebels make use of the distraction, their movements synchronized like a well-rehearsed dance. Grace signals with a subtle hand gesture, and they seamlessly dissolve into the shadows, taking routes that the guards' attention cannot follow.

As the last echoes of Natalie's conversation fade, the guards remain oblivious to the rebels' departure. The palace's opulent halls swallow the rebels, their heartbeats echoing in rhythm with the pulse of their mission. As the rebels ventured deeper into the palace's core, the grand halls unfolded before them like a testament to opulence. Glistening chandeliers hung from ornate ceilings, casting shimmering reflections upon marble floors. Elaborate tapestries depicted scenes of prosperity and unity—deliberate illusions crafted to pacify the masses while concealing the regime's true nature. The walls of these grand halls were adorned with intricate carvings and gold leaf, a stark contrast to the crumbling reality beyond the palace walls. Portraits of the regime's leaders stared down, their impassive gaze a constant reminder of the suffering endured by those who dared oppose them. Each step taken by the rebels echoed through the cavernous spaces, a silent reminder that they tread upon the domain of the corrupt.

Ethan's grip on the chain around his neck tightened—a tangible reminder of his purpose and the weight of his father's and New Eden's hopes. The resolute expressions of his companions reflected their shared understanding—they were not here merely to infiltrate, but to expose the festering corruption that lay beneath this facade of luxury. Their journey led them through labyrinthine corridors, each turn revealing more of the palace's grandeur. Gilded banisters framed staircases that seemed to stretch into infinity, while stained glass windows depicted idyllic scenes that masked the true state of the world. The rebels remained vigilant, cautious of any guards or surveillance that could compromise their mission. At last, they arrived at a seemingly innocuous chamber, its entrance blending seamlessly with the opulent décor. Yet, an air of secrecy hung about it, as if the room itself held its breath, guarding the secrets concealed within. Thomas, drawing from his past experiences within the palace, recognized this as the entryway to the clandestine chamber they sought.

Ethan's heart raced as he studied the unassuming room. It was devoid of grandeur, unlike the ostentatious displays that characterized the rest of the palace. The chamber's walls were adorned with faded murals, depicting scenes that appeared almost ordinary—until one looked closer. Hidden within the brushstrokes were symbols and codes that hinted at a deeper, concealed purpose. Grace stepped forward, her eyes narrowing as she examined the chamber with a cautious curiosity. "This is it," she whispered, her voice echoing in the silence. "This is where the truth lies, where we unveil the secrets that have plagued New Eden."

With her guidance, the rebels began a meticulous search of the room. They pressed their hands against the walls, tapped on the floorboards, and studied the murals with an investigator's scrutiny. Slowly, a pattern emerged—the faint outlines of a concealed door that blended seamlessly into the mural. Evelyn, with a combination of careful analysis and her ingenious intuition, discovered the mechanism that unlocked the hidden passage. A section of the mural slid away noiselessly, revealing a narrow stairwell that descended into darkness—an invitation to confront the past and expose the treachery that had tainted New Eden's origins. Their resolve hardened, and the rebels shared a silent nod of understanding before descending into the depths of the hidden chamber.

As the rebels descend into the hidden chamber, a hushed tension hangs in the air. The dim light casts eerie shadows on the walls, and ancient symbols, intricately etched into the stone, emerge from the darkness. The symbols tell a story of secrecy, power, and a twisted ambition that once thrived within these very walls. Each curve and line seems to whisper of a past that's been buried, a past the rebels are determined to unveil. The chamber itself exudes an unsettling aura—an amalgamation of opulence and decay. Golden ornaments, once gleaming, now tarnished by time, adorn the room. Tapestries depicting scenes of grandeur hang askew as if reflecting the twisted ideals of those who once gathered here. Flickering torches cast dancing shadows, giving life to the ancient symbols that line the walls like sentinels of forgotten truths. In the heart of the chamber, a pedestal rises—a stark contrast to the room's decayed grandeur. Upon it rests an encrypted device, a futuristic fusion of technology and elegance. Lights dance across its surface, illuminating its sleek design. It pulses with almost palpable energy, a promise of hidden knowledge and revelations waiting to be unlocked.

Evelyn steps forward, her eyes fixated on the device. Her fingers dance over its surface as she scans its enigmatic symbols and interfaces. Her lips curve into a determined smile, her expertise in engineering and decryption coming to the forefront. She recognizes the device's intricate encryption mechanisms and realizes that within its code lies the key to unraveling the faction's darkest secrets. But their progress is halted by an unexpected intrusion—a chilling silence followed by the sound of footsteps echoing through the chamber. Shadows shift, revealing figures clad in dark attire—the remnants of Dr. Collins' faction. Their eyes gleam with a mixture of resentment and desperation, as if guarding the legacy of betrayal they had once sought to realize.

The room becomes a battleground of tension, the rebels facing off against their adversaries. Captain Grace's hand tightens around her weapon, her gaze unwavering as she locks eyes with the faction's leader. The rebels sense the weight of history pressing upon them—the echoes of a past conflict, now reignited. Ethan's fingers instinctively clutch the chain around his neck, the symbol of his father's presence and the promise of unity. His father stands by his side, a silent pillar of strength. The rebels are prepared to confront not just the faction but the shadows of their pasts, each step forward a testament to their commitment to justice and hope. A silence hangs heavy, broken only by the crackling of torches and the low hum of the encrypted device.

CHAPTER SIXTEEN

The Battle Begins

The hidden chamber crackles with an electric tension that seems to permeate the very air. The room, once a well-kept secret, now hosts a collision of fates. Ethereal shadows dance upon the stone walls, their movement mirroring the conflicting emotions that simmer beneath the surface. The torchlight flickers erratically, casting fleeting glimmers of illumination upon the faces of those gathered within. Ethan stands at the forefront, his presence commanding even in the face of uncertainty. His eyes, normally alive with curiosity and determination, now hold a fiery intensity. As he steps forward, the echoes of his footsteps seem to resonate like a heartbeat—a rhythm of purpose that reverberates through the chamber. The rebels and the remnants of Dr. Collins' faction lock eyes, their stares a clash of wills and ideals. It's a moment that encapsulates the battle of past and future, of oppression and liberation. In the flickering light, Ethan's gaze narrows, his jaw clenched in unwavering resolve.

He draws a deep breath, his voice rising from within, a quiet yet unyielding force that cuts through the tension. Ethan said "We are here to reclaim the truth, to unveil the secrets that have festered within New Eden's heart. For too long, darkness has shrouded our sanctuary, its purpose twisted and tainted. Today, we stand not just for ourselves, but for all those who have suffered under the weight of deception." His words hang in the air like an unspoken oath—a pledge to unravel the lies and reclaim the promise of hope that New Eden was meant to embody. The chamber's walls seem to absorb his determination, each stone bearing witness to the courage that drives him forward. As the final echoes of Ethan's words fade, a palpable tension grips the room. The rebels and the faction's remnants stand on opposing sides, divided not just by space but by ideals—a chasm that has grown wider with each hidden truth and each unspoken betrayal.

The torches continue their dance, casting fleeting shadows upon Ethan's face as he meets the gaze of his father, Thomas Foster. There's a shared understanding in their eyes—a silent exchange of strength and purpose. It's a reminder that their fight isn't just for New Eden, but for the legacy of those who believed in a sanctuary of rebirth. In the charged silence that follows, the rebels and the faction remain locked in a battle of wills, a precursor to the larger conflict that awaits them. The chamber seems to hold its breath, a silent witness to the clash between the echoes of a dark past and the flicker of a brighter future. And as the tension lingers, the rebels ready themselves for the battle that will determine the fate of New Eden and the world beyond its walls.

Grace's voice cuts through the charged air of the hidden chamber, her words igniting a spark of determination in the eyes of every rebel present. Today," she declares, her tone unwavering, "we stand united against the darkness that has clouded our world for far too long. We fight not just for ourselves, but for every person who's ever looked up at the sky and dared to dream of a brighter future. We fight for justice, for a future where New Eden can rise as a sanctuary of hope once more." Her eyes, deep pools of unwavering resolve, sweep across the faces of her comrades. Ethan stands by her side, his gaze locked onto Grace, their shared purpose unspoken but deeply understood. Around them, the rebels exchange glances of fierce determination, acknowledging the weight of the battle they're about to face. With a shared nod that communicates more than words ever could, the rebels and the remnants of Dr. Collins' faction brace themselves for the storm that's about to be unleashed. The chamber seems to hold its breath, the silence pregnant with the impending clash of ideals.

And then, the first strike is unleashed, shattering the stillness. A faction member lunges at a rebel, their clash symbolizing the deep-seated conflict between the past that sought control and the future that yearned for freedom. Metal clashes against metal, the ring of steel echoing in the chamber. Gunfire follows, sparking chaos as rebels and guards alike exchange shots, each shot fired carrying the echoes of an age-old struggle. Ethan is in the thick of it, his movements fluid and precise as he engages an opponent. His years surviving the decaying city have honed his instincts, and his determination fuels every strike. Memories of his father's absence and the secrets buried within New Eden add an extra edge to his resolve. The weight of his shared mission with his comrades propels him forward, driving him to clash with unmatched fervor.

Around him, the rebels fight with a shared fire, their eyes set on a vision of a reimagined future. Evelyn's ingenious devices create pockets of advantage, Thomas moves with a calculated grace, using the terrain to his advantage, and Natalie's diplomatic finesse helps shift the odds in their favor. The chamber transforms into a battleground of ideals and action, the embodiment of a world teetering on the edge of transformation. As blows are exchanged and bullets fly, the clash of opposing ideals reverberates through the grand halls of the palace. Each move, each action taken by the rebels is a testament to their unwavering belief in a world free from deception and tyranny. With every swing of a weapon, they fight not only against the faction but against the legacy of a past that sought to stifle the very essence of hope.

Amid the swirling chaos of battle, a moment of profound connection unfolds. In the heart of the palace's grand corridors, amidst the clash of weapons and the echoes of determination, stands Ethan and his father, Thomas. Their eyes lock, each gaze carrying a multitude of unspoken emotions—pride, love, and the weight of their shared purpose. The torchlight flickers across their faces, casting dancing shadows that seem to mirror the dance of hope and adversity within their hearts. Side by side, father and son fight as if their very souls are entwined, their movements fluid and synchronized, a testament to the bond that transcends time and circumstance.

Thomas' seasoned expertise and Ethan's youthful determination form a formidable partnership. Their strikes are measured, each action infused with intention. It's not just a battle against the physical adversaries—they're fighting to redefine the legacy that New Eden will carry, to strip away the layers of deception that have obscured its true purpose. With each strike that lands, with every act of defiance, the rebels draw closer to their goal. The chamber's secrets are no longer shrouded in darkness; they shimmer with the promise of revelation. Evelyn's fingers dance over the encrypted device, her skillful manipulation gradually unlocking its hidden truths. The device pulses with an otherworldly glow, a beacon of knowledge amidst the chaos.

Around them, the battle rages on. The palace's opulent walls, once a symbol of power, now bear witness to a transformation—a transformation born from the courage of those who dare to challenge oppression. Guards loyal to the regime fall one by one, their resolve waning in the face of the rebels' unyielding spirit. The faction's remnants, once staunch defenders of a twisted cause, falter as they face the united front of the rebels. Ethan's eyes meet those of the faction's leader, a silent exchange that speaks volumes. It's a confrontation not just between individuals, but between two divergent paths—one driven by greed and control, the other by hope and freedom.

In the midst of the chaos, Ethan and Thomas share fleeting words, their breathless exchanges fueling the fire of determination burning within them. Their voices cut through the sounds of combat, a reminder that this battle is more than just a clash of weapons—it's a reclamation of purpose, a rewriting of history, and a catalyst for change. As Evelyn's fingers complete their intricate dance, the encrypted device hums with a final surge of energy.

The secrets of the chamber are laid bare—the truth of New Eden's origins, the faction's treachery, and the path forward. And as the battle reaches its crescendo, a transformative realization dawns upon Ethan. This fight, this struggle—it's not just about defeating the regime and exposing the faction. It's about breathing life into the vision that inspired New Eden, about ensuring that it becomes a haven where humanity can truly heal and thrive. With a final surge of determination, the rebels push forward, their rallying cries resonating through the palace's corridors. As strikes land and the chamber's secrets unravel, a new future emerges—one bathed in the light of hope and justice, where the legacy of betrayal is overshadowed by the promise of renewal.

CHAPTER SEVENTEEN

Sacrifices and Losses

Amidst the swirling chaos of battle, the very air seems to thicken with the weight of sacrifice and determination. The grand corridors of the palace, once adorned with opulence, now bear witness to a clash of ideals—a collision of forces that have converged in a struggle for the soul of New Eden. The symphony of conflict is composed of clashes, shouts, and the rhythmic pulse of footfalls—the harmonious chaos of a rebellion ignited. The clash of weapons creates a dissonant melody that echoes through the palace's halls, each clash a testament to the rebels' unwavering spirit. The chorus of shouts—some fueled by anger, some by grief, all by unyielding determination—melds into a battle cry that reverberates through the very foundations of the palace.

In the heart of it all stands Ethan, a figure of both vulnerability and indomitable resolve. His eyes, reflecting a mixture of pain and purpose, scan the battlefield with an acute awareness. He's not just leading a rebellion; he's leading a movement—a movement that seeks to unearth the truth buried beneath layers of deception. The palace's grand corridors, once adorned with gilded decorations, have become the backdrop for a struggle that will shape the course of history. The walls themselves seem to absorb the echoes of combat, witnessing the conflict between a regime desperate to maintain control and a rebellion fueled by the dream of a better world.

As guards loyal to the oppressive regime clash with the remnants of Dr. Collins' faction, the air is charged with desperation. These adversaries, once divided by their conflicting ideals, now stand united in their fear of losing power. Swords clash, gunfire echoes, and sparks dance in the air as the battle blazes on. The palace's once pristine tapestries hang askew, symbols of the shattered illusions that the regime has woven to conceal its true nature. Marble pillars, once symbols of strength, now bear the scars of conflict. The very architecture of the palace seems to cry out—a visual testament to the transformation taking place.

Amidst the chaotic dance of combat, Ethan and his father, Thomas, stand shoulder to shoulder—a united front against the regime's forces. The echoes of clashing weapons and desperate shouts form a symphony of resistance, each note underscoring the unbreakable bond between father and son. Their movements are a reflection of their connection—an unspoken language of shared purpose and unyielding resolve. Thomas' experienced maneuvers complement Ethan's youthful energy, a testament to the legacy of a father who taught his son not just how to fight, but why to fight.

The palace's grand corridors become a canvas of conflict, the rebels pushing forward against waves of opposition. Amidst the cacophony of battle, the palpable connection between Ethan and his father serves as a beacon of inspiration, a symbol of hope for a world reborn from the ashes. But the tides of battle are fickle, and fate takes a cruel turn. In a moment of vulnerability, as the chaos swirls around them, a single misstep is all it takes. Thomas' valiant defense falters, a fraction of a second too late, and the clash of steel against steel echoes with a finality that hangs heavy in the air.

Time seems to slow as Ethan watches, helpless, as his father's form crumples to the ground—a stark contrast to the strength that once emanated from him. The world blurs around Ethan, and his heart clenches with a mixture of disbelief and agony. In that heart-wrenching instant, a hero's journey comes to a tragic end, and a pillar of strength is taken from the world. The pain of loss ripples through the ranks of the rebels. Grief becomes a silent companion amidst the battle cries, the weight of sacrifice settling upon their shoulders. Ethan's father, a man who had fought not just for a cause but for a vision of renewal, now rests among the fallen. Ethan's voice breaks through the din, a cry that resonates with sorrow.

A maelstrom of emotions swirled within Ethan, yet sorrow seemed to engulf everything else. There was no anger, no vengeful roar against the injustice of the moment—just a raw and profound ache that reverberated through his very being. The battle around him became a distant hum, a backdrop to his private grief, as he gazed upon his fallen father. In the moments that followed, Ethan's movements were almost automatic, as if his body was guided by a force beyond his control. He knelt beside his father, his fingers trembling as they brushed against the cooling skin. He wanted to reach out, to shake his father awake, to beg for another moment—to somehow reverse the course of events that had led to this heart-wrenching loss.

But reality was unyielding, and the truth remained. Ethan's father was gone, a hero fallen in the pursuit of justice. The dream they had shared, the vision of a renewed world, now felt both distant and fragile, as if it had been torn from his grasp. The tears that had threatened earlier finally spilled over, tracing a path down Ethan's cheeks. He didn't try to stop them, nor did he attempt to suppress the sobs that wracked his body. The pain of loss was too great to be contained—a torrent of grief that demanded to be released.

Around him, the battle raged on, but it was as if the world had faded into the background. All that mattered, all that held significance in that moment, was the void left by his father's absence. Ethan's vision blurred, his father's memory a bittersweet ache that pulsed within his chest. As the battle's echoes gradually seeped back into his awareness, Ethan found himself surrounded by his comrades—those who had stood by his side, who had shared in the pain of loss. Their faces were a reflection of his own grief, their eyes mirrors of sorrow. Grace's voice broke through the haze, her tone a mix of compassion and unwavering support.

Grace: "Ethan, we mourn with you. But we must continue the fight—for your father, for all those who've sacrificed. We must make sure their sacrifices were not in vain." Ethan's gaze lifted from his father's still form to meet Grace's eyes. In her expression, he saw a reflection of the resolve he had lost in his grief. His sorrow, his pain—it was shared by those around him. And as their voices joined together in a chorus of determination, Ethan felt a spark of something other than sorrow—something akin to his father's unwavering commitment. He wiped away his tears, his expression a mix of sadness and newfound resolve. The battle, the fight—it wasn't just about him anymore. It was about honoring his father's memory, about rewriting history, about reclaiming New Eden's vision. As he stood, his shoulders squared and his heart heavy but unbroken, Ethan took a tentative step forward—a step towards embracing the pain of loss as a driving force for change, a force that would shape the world anew.

As the echoes of grief and determination filled the air, a transformation ignited within Ethan—a transformation that went beyond the physical realm. It was as if the weight of his emotions had birthed a dormant power, a force that surged through his veins with an intensity that matched the fire in his heart. His eyes, once clouded with sorrow, blazed with an otherworldly light, a reflection of the power that had awoken within him. The air crackled with energy, a prelude to the storm that was about to be unleashed. The rebels, his comrades, watched in awe and trepidation, sensing that something extraordinary was unfolding.

Ethan's form seemed to shimmer, his presence a fusion of human and something more. A surge of energy radiated outward, a force that pushed back the encroaching shadows of grief and despair. The ground trembled beneath his feet as he took a step forward, the very earth acknowledging the awakening power within him. The remnants of Dr. Collins' faction stood frozen, their faces etched with a mixture of fear and disbelief. Their weapons wavered, their resolve faltering in the face of this new and unprecedented force. They had witnessed loss, but they were unprepared for the cataclysmic shift that was about to occur.

Ethan's hands lifted, his fingers dancing with an intricate weave of energy and determination. The air shimmered around him, a maelstrom of power that responded to his very will. With a primal roar that echoed through the palace's grand halls, he unleashed the force within him—a force that tore through the fabric of reality itself. The very ground shook as waves of energy radiated outward from Ethan, an unstoppable torrent that struck the faction with the force of a cosmic storm. Walls shattered, debris flew, and a tempest of power engulfed the remnants of the faction. They were helpless before the onslaught, their resistance reduced to nothingness in the face of Ethan's unleashed power.

Amidst the chaos, one figure remained standing—the last surviving member of the faction. He trembled, his defiance eclipsed by the overwhelming force that Ethan had become. As the air crackled and pulsed, the figure found his voice—a desperate plea for mercy.

Faction Member: (voice quivering) "Please... spare me. I'll tell you anything, anything you want to know."

Ethan's power began to recede, his aura of energy diminishing as quickly as it had appeared. His eyes, still ablaze with an intensity beyond human comprehension, fixed upon the figure before him. With a gesture of his hand, the air itself seemed to twist, binding the figure in an ethereal grip that defied the laws of nature.

Ethan: (voice echoing with power) "Tell me, then. Tell me where Dr. Collins is."

The figure's voice shook as he revealed the information, his words carrying a weight of desperation and the knowledge of the futility of resistance.

Faction Member: (voice trembling) "He... He's in the heart of New Eden. The control center, hidden deep below the surface."

With a final gesture, Ethan released his grip on the figure. The air returned to its normal state, the palace's grand halls echoing with the aftermath of the unleashed power. As the dust settled, Ethan's gaze remained fixed on the figure, a testament to the change that had overcome him—the change that had unlocked a force within him beyond his understanding. Ethan's power had revealed itself, an embodiment of his grief, his determination, and his unwavering commitment to his cause. The remnants of Dr. Collins' faction had been defeated, and the last piece of the puzzle—the location of Dr. Collins—had been uncovered. With a newfound resolve burning in his eyes, Ethan turned and took a step forward, his path clear and his purpose defined. The battle had taken its toll, but from the ashes of loss, a phoenix had risen—a force of change, an embodiment of hope, and a catalyst for a future yet to be written.

CHAPTER EIGHTEEN

Confrontation

The journey into the heart of New Eden was a descent into a world of mystery and uncertainty. The rebels traversed through labyrinthine passageways, each turn taking them deeper into the bowels of the city. The corridors seemed to echo with the whispers of history, the hushed voices of those who had walked these paths before, leaving their imprint on the walls. Forgotten chambers yawned open as they ventured forward, their entrances hidden in plain sight, a testament to the skill with which the city's secrets had been concealed. The rebels pressed on, a flicker of torchlight casting elongated shadows on the walls that seemed to dance in rhythm with their steps. The air was thick with anticipation, a tension that mirrored the weight of their purpose.

As they navigated through the hidden depths, the walls themselves seemed to tell a story—an intricate tapestry of symbols and engravings that spoke of a history both grand and enigmatic. Carvings of unity and progress adorned the stone, juxtaposed with more cryptic markings that hinted at the darker underbelly of New Eden's past. Each image seemed to carry the weight of time, a narrative etched into the very foundation of the city. Torches lined the corridors, their flames casting a warm, flickering glow that painted the walls in shifting shades of gold and amber. But amidst this illumination, shadows danced—a silent reminder that even amidst the light, truths could remain hidden. The torchlight caught the faint glimmers of symbols etched into the walls, each one a puzzle piece in the grand narrative of New Eden.

The air grew heavy with the scent of age and secrecy, each breath carrying with it a sense of anticipation and unease. It was as if the very walls were alive, bearing witness to the rebels' journey—a journey that would culminate in a confrontation with the enigmatic figure at the heart of the city's transformation. Every step forward was a step into the unknown, a step closer to the culmination of their quest. The rebels moved with a sense of purpose, driven by the desire to unveil the truth that had been shrouded in layers of deception. The journey through hidden passageways and forgotten chambers was not just a physical progression, but a descent into the core of New Eden's history—a history waiting to be uncovered, rewritten, and reclaimed.

Amidst the blend of ancient engravings and futuristic technologies, the rebels arrive at their destination—an awe-inspiring grand chamber that appears to breathe with an ethereal light. The walls seem to shift and shimmer, reflecting a tapestry of images that hint at the layers of history that have unfolded within these hallowed halls. Torches line the periphery, casting flickering shadows that dance across the walls like spectral memories. At the heart of this chamber, an almost spectral figure stands—an embodiment of both authority and enigma. Dr. Samuel Collins, a man whose very presence commands attention, exudes an aura of authority that's inescapable. His form seems to meld with the ambient light, casting an enigmatic silhouette that echoes the dichotomy of New Eden itself.

As Ethan's gaze meets Dr. Collins', a current of understanding passes between them—a recognition of shared truths that transcends the clash of ideologies. The weight of their pasts—of choices made and paths diverged—settles between them like a palpable presence, a silent narrative that hangs heavy in the air. In this charged moment, the memory of Thomas Foster stands as a bridge between the two figures—a symbol of both unity and division. The memory of a man whose ideals had shaped Ethan's convictions and whose sacrifice had ignited the rebel's spirit. The loss of Eden, Dr. Collins' daughter, forms a parallel narrative—an undercurrent of tragedy that underscores the choices that have led them to this precipice.

Dr. Collins' eyes hold a myriad of emotions—an amalgamation of conviction, regret, and an unwavering belief in his cause. Ethan's gaze, on the other hand, reflects a mixture of sorrow and determination—a resolve strengthened by the weight of his father's legacy. In this unspoken exchange, their destinies align in a moment that feels both fateful and inevitable. The chamber, a crucible of past and present, pulses with a resonance that speaks to the significance of this confrontation. The echoes of history seem to swirl in the air—a chorus of voices that demand acknowledgment, a reckoning with the choices that have shaped New Eden's trajectory. As the silence lingers, the tension between them palpable, the chamber becomes a canvas upon which the battle of ideologies will unfold.

Dr. Collins' voice resonates through the chamber, carrying a weight of experience that colors every word he speaks.

Dr. Collins: "Welcome to the heart of New Eden, where dreams and realities intertwine. You seek answers, but do you truly comprehend the weight of the truths that have been hidden from you?"

His words hang in the air, a question that lingers like a specter—a question that demands reflection, not just from the rebels, but from Dr. Collins himself. His gaze, unyielding and piercing, seems to hold secrets untold, locked within the recesses of his memories.

Ethan's response carries a sense of unwavering resolve, a reflection of the shared purpose that binds the rebels together.

Ethan: "We seek the truth, not just for ourselves, but for all those who've suffered and all those who've believed in New Eden's promise. You may have built this city, but the foundation was laid by ideals that transcended your ambitions."

The tension in the chamber becomes palpable, the space between Dr. Collins and Ethan a battleground of ideologies. Dr. Collins' gaze shifts, his eyes passing over each rebel with a mixture of appraisal and acknowledgment. His conviction remains unshaken, even as his gaze softens with a hint of pain.

Dr. Collins: "New Eden was meant to be a sanctuary—a place to heal, to renew, to rebuild. But the loss of my daughter Eden... it drove me to harness the city's potential for power, to shape it in ways that would prevent such loss from ever occurring again."

As he utters his daughter's name, a shadow seems to pass over the chamber—a shadow of a loss so profound that it resonates through time. The rebels listen, their expressions a blend of empathy and determination, each face reflecting the experiences of pain that have shaped their journey.

Ethan's voice carries the weight of truth, as he speaks not just for himself, but for the dreams that have been twisted by Dr. Collins' actions.

Ethan: "Loss has touched us all. But the path you chose—the path of control and manipulation—it's not the legacy New Eden deserves. You turned a sanctuary into a regime, a vision into a facade."

Dr. Collins' gaze remains unflinching, his stance a testament to the conviction that has driven his choices. The clash of ideologies reverberates, a storm of beliefs colliding in the heart of New Eden—a reflection of the larger struggle that has brought them to this moment.

Dr. Collins: "I sought to prevent loss, to ensure a future without pain. But perhaps I lost sight of the true essence of New Eden—a place where humanity could find solace, where dreams could flourish."

As the words escape his lips, a veil seems to lift, revealing the depths of his own conflict. He hesitates, as if grappling with the weight of his past choices—the choices that have led to a city divided, a vision tainted by power, and the legacy of a daughter lost.

Dr. Collins: (voice heavy with emotion) "My daughter, Eden... She was the heart of my world. Her loss was a void I could never fill. It was in the depths of that grief that the idea took shape—the notion that by controlling every aspect of New Eden, I could prevent others from feeling that pain."

The chamber's silence seems to absorb his words, the tragedy of Eden's loss casting shadows over the present. The rebels' expressions remain a mix of empathy and resolve, a testament to the shared experiences that have shaped their journey.

Ethan's voice, firm yet tinged with understanding, rises once more.

Ethan: "Dr. Collins, we acknowledge your pain, your grief. But we cannot allow that pain to justify the path you've chosen. The essence of New Eden, its promise, is greater than any single individual's ambitions."

Dr. Collins' eyes seem to hold a storm of conflicting emotions—a maelstrom of regret, pain, and the lingering conviction that has fueled his actions.

Dr. Collins: (voice tinged with bitterness) "You speak of the essence of New Eden, but do you truly understand what that essence entails? A sanctuary, a safe haven—it's a noble ideal, but it's also a fragile one. The world outside is unforgiving, relentless in its cruelty. I sought to shield those within these walls from the horrors I've witnessed, from the heartache that tore my own world apart."

Ethan's voice remains steady, a counterpoint to the turmoil that Dr. Collins' words evoke.

Ethan: "Shielding them from pain by wielding power isn't the same as healing. It's a path paved with good intentions, yes, but one that ultimately leads to oppression and a loss of freedom. People should have the right to forge their own destinies, even in the face of adversity."

Dr. Collins' gaze is fixed on Ethan, his eyes a reflection of a lifetime of choices, each thread woven with the intent to reshape a world scarred by loss.

Dr. Collins: "You're idealistic, young Ethan. But you've yet to witness the world's true darkness—the depths of despair that can consume even the strongest of souls. My intentions may have strayed, but they were rooted in the belief that control could prevent the suffering I've endured."

Ethan's expression remains unyielding, his voice unwavering as he addresses the core of their clash.

Ethan: "Control doesn't prevent suffering, Dr. Collins. It merely replaces one form of suffering with another. Freedom carries risks, but it also carries the potential for growth, for healing, and for a future worth fighting for."

The chamber seems to hold its breath, the clash of beliefs echoing off the walls—a symphony of conflict and conviction, each note resonating with the experiences that have brought them to this moment.

Dr. Collins: (voice softened) "You speak with a conviction that reminds me of myself in my youth—the idealism, the unwavering belief in a better world. But ideals can crumble when faced with the realities of a world that refuses to yield."

Ethan's gaze meets Dr. Collins', his eyes holding a mix of determination and empathy.

Ethan: "It's true that the world can be cruel, but it's also capable of resilience and redemption. We've seen it in the midst of chaos, in the strength of communities that rise from the ashes. New Eden was meant to embody that resilience, not suppress it."

Dr. Collins' shoulders sag slightly, the weight of his choices becoming more evident with each exchange of words.

Dr. Collins: (voice tinged with regret) "Perhaps I've clung to control for too long, blinded by the illusion of protection. The city's foundation was built on hope, and I've twisted it into something unrecognizable. But can you truly believe that reclaiming that essence is possible, that redemption is within reach?"

Ethan's voice carries a sense of hope that transcends the boundaries of doubt.

Ethan: "We believe in the power of change, in the strength of unity. Dr. Collins, your choices shaped New Eden, but they don't define its destiny. It's never too late to rewrite a legacy—to rebuild a sanctuary that stands as a beacon of renewal, not repression."

The air between them seems to shift, a space charged with the weight of their convictions. In that charged silence, the battle of ideologies rages—a battle that will determine the fate of New Eden and the future it holds for humanity.

As the echoes of their conversation fade, the chamber remains a crucible of beliefs, a proving ground for the clash of perspectives. In the heart of New Eden, amidst the confrontation of past and present, a path forward becomes clearer—a path that hinges on the choices of individuals and the resilience of a world yearning to heal.

The tension in the chamber begins to dissipate as the weight of their conversation lingers in the air. Dr. Samuel Collins stands at the precipice of a decision—a decision that could reshape the destiny of New Eden and restore the vision that had once ignited its creation.

Dr. Collins: (voice filled with resolution) "Ethan, you've reminded me of the ideals that laid the foundation of New Eden. My grief, my pursuit of control—it's led us down a path I never intended. It's time to reclaim this city's true purpose, to rebuild it as a sanctuary where humanity can thrive."

Ethan's gaze meets Dr. Collins', his eyes reflecting a mix of hope and cautious optimism.

Ethan: "It's not too late, Dr. Collins. New Eden can still be a place of healing, renewal, and unity. But it will require us to confront the mistakes of the past and embrace a future that is shaped by the collective efforts of those who believe in its potential."

Dr. Collins nods, his gaze shifting to the chamber's walls—the symbols and echoes of a history that had been distorted but not irreparably damaged.

Dr. Collins: "We'll start by dismantling the mechanisms of control, by empowering the residents to have a voice in the decisions that shape their lives. We'll rebuild the city's infrastructure to support growth, learning from our past mistakes."

Ethan: "And the survivors who've fought alongside us?"

Dr. Collins' gaze meets Ethan's with a newfound sense of shared purpose.

Dr. Collins: "They will be the torchbearers of this new beginning. We'll extend an invitation to all survivors, to those who yearn for a better life and are willing to contribute to a community where hope and progress flourish."

As their conversation unfolds, the realization dawns—the echoes of their confrontation have given rise to a resolution that transcends personal agendas. Dr. Collins' transformation is a reflection of the resilience of the human spirit, the capacity to change and to adapt in the face of truth.

CHAPTER NINETEEN

New Eden

People from beyond the city's borders, who had once been excluded and denied the sanctuary that New Eden promised, arrive at its gates with hesitant hope. Their faces bear the marks of a world outside that has tested their strength and resolve. But as the gates swing open, their uncertainty is met with warm smiles, welcoming hands, and the promise of a fresh start. Families torn apart by circumstances find themselves wrapped in tearful embraces, their reunions a testament to the healing power of unity. Loved ones who had been separated by fate are now reunited under the banner of a city redefined by compassion. Stories spill forth like precious gems, exchanged with laughter and tears, a reminder that the human spirit is bound by shared experiences.

The city's once-divided streets are now a canvas of collaboration and coexistence. Strangers, once separated by suspicion, become friends linked by common purpose. Individuals from different walks of life join hands in a dance of renewal, their diversity becoming a source of strength rather than division. The clamor of hammers and the mechanical hum of construction equipment fill the air, a symphony of progress that echoes through the city's revitalized corridors. The rhythm of work becomes a symbol of transformation—a chorus of determination that underscores the collective effort to rebuild what was lost.

Streets that were once lined with propaganda and reminders of oppression are cleansed of their tainted history. In their place, vibrant murals blossom, depicting scenes of unity, resilience, and the beauty of a world reborn. Every brushstroke becomes a declaration of the city's renewal, each stroke of color a testament to the ability to reimagine a brighter future. Artisans, fueled by inspiration and the desire to mend what had been broken, infuse the city with their creativity. Sculptures rise from forgotten corners, telling stories of struggle and triumph. Gardens flourish with the careful cultivation of life, their blooms reflecting the hope that blossoms in the hearts of New Eden's residents.

The city's architecture, once a cold manifestation of control, begins to reflect the aspirations of its people. Buildings are adorned with intricate carvings and vibrant mosaics, each telling a story of unity and shared purpose. Parks are transformed into communal spaces where laughter and camaraderie flow freely. The clang of hammers and the symphony of construction become a backdrop to everyday life, a reminder that progress is both tangible and ongoing. And as the sun sets, casting a warm glow over the city, the transformation is illuminated. New Eden stands as a living testament to the power of renewal, an embodiment of the capacity for change that resides within the human spirit.

Ethan and Sarah, their eyes reflecting the weight of their shared loss, find solace amidst the bustling activity of rebuilding. The once desolate streets now teem with life—people carrying tools, painting walls, and sharing knowing glances that hold the promise of a brighter future.

In the evenings, as the sun dips below the horizon, the city transforms into a sea of flickering lights. Candles are placed on windowsills and doorsteps, their gentle flames illuminating the faces of those who gather to remember their loved ones. The soft glow casts a warm embrace over the city, a reminder that even in the face of darkness, there is always light.

Stories are shared, passed from person to person like cherished heirlooms. Tales of bravery and sacrifice intertwine with anecdotes of everyday life, creating a tapestry of remembrance that stretches through time. Laughter mingles with tears, and in the midst of it all, a profound sense of unity emerges—an unspoken understanding that each person's story is a thread woven into the fabric of New Eden's renewal.

Ethan and Sarah, though burdened by their own grief, find solace in the collective mourning. Their hands hold candles, the soft flames flickering like stars in the night sky, a symbolic connection to the loved ones they've lost. Their presence is a reminder that pain can be a unifying force, forging bonds that transcend words.

As raindrops fall, they mingle with tears—the rain acting as a cleansing veil, washing away the residue of sorrow and leaving room for growth. Each tear seems to carry a fragment of the city's collective grief, and with each tear shed, a renewed determination to shape a world that honors the past while embracing the future takes root.

Through the city's mourning, a sense of purpose emerges—a commitment to carry the memory of the fallen forward, to ensure that their sacrifices were not in vain. And amidst the candles, the stories, and the shared tears, there emerges a glimmer of hope—a spark that ignites the journey of healing and redemption.

Ethan's presence amidst the bustling streets of the renewed New Eden is a quiet testament to the power of resilience. His steps are purposeful, his demeanor a reflection of both the burdens he carries and the determination that propels him forward. Every glance he shares with a passing resident, every nod of acknowledgment, is a reassurance that the city's transformation is a collective effort, a journey undertaken together.

As the city's buildings rise from the ground, they carry with them the echoes of a shared vision—a vision that transcends the confines of power and control. Parks burst forth with vibrant flowers, their colors a vivid reminder of the beauty that can emerge even from the harshest of environments. Children laugh as they chase each other through open spaces, their laughter mingling with the soft rustle of leaves and the distant hum of construction.

Market stalls line the streets, each one a window into the diverse talents of the city's people. Artisans display their creations—jewelry, sculptures, paintings—each piece a testament to the creativity that thrives in a world unburdened by oppression. The scent of freshly baked goods mingles with the aroma of spices, a reminder that life's simple pleasures can be celebrated even in the face of adversity.

The heart of New Eden, once a cold and imposing symbol of control, now beats with the warmth of unity. Music floats through the air, its melodies echoing through alleys and avenues. Musicians gather in open squares, playing instruments that had long been silenced. Their music is a symphony of renewal, a harmonious reminder that even amidst struggle, humanity can create beauty.

In the evenings, as the sun sets in a blaze of orange and gold, lanterns illuminate the city's streets, casting a warm and inviting glow. Families gather in plazas to share meals, to share stories, and to share the simple joy of companionship. The city has become a tapestry of lives woven together—each thread a unique story, each individual a vital part of the whole.

And amidst it all stands Ethan, his gaze reflective and unwavering. His heart carries the weight of loss, the memory of his father ever present. But it also carries the spark of hope—a hope that has been kindled by the resilience of the city, by the bonds forged through struggle and triumph.

The walls of the once somber chamber have undergone a transformation, echoing the city's own journey of rebirth. Murals now grace the surfaces, each stroke of paint depicting the evolution from oppression to liberation. Vivid scenes capture the spirit of the rebellion—the rebels standing tall against tyranny, the unity that brought down walls of control, and the collective resilience that turned the tide.

The ancient symbols, once cryptic reminders of a darker era, have been lovingly repurposed. They now tell a tale of hope, tracing a path of transformation etched into the very fabric of New Eden's foundation. These symbols now bear witness to the city's reclamation of its true essence, serving as a visual reminder of the power of change.

Ethan and Sarah, their steps carrying the weight of their shared loss, find themselves embraced by the warmth of a newfound family. They've become more than just survivors of a battle; they've become beacons of hope amidst the city's rejuvenation. In the midst of their own healing, their stories become intertwined with those around them; stories of courage, resilience, and the unwavering pursuit of a brighter future.

As the sun dips below the horizon, casting a cascade of warm hues across the renewed city, the streets come alive with a soft glow. Lanterns are lit, each one a beacon of light that mirrors the city's own journey from darkness to illumination. The air is filled with laughter and the distant strains of music, a chorus that fills the heart with a sense of unity.

Ethan stands on a rooftop, his gaze sweeping over the expanse of the city. The soft glow of lanterns paints a tapestry of light, transforming the city into a canvas of dreams fulfilled. In this moment, amidst the shared stories and the echoes of the past, he finds a sense of hope—a hope that transcends the trials and tribulations, a hope that stands as a testament to the enduring strength of the human spirit.

The city's rebirth is a celebration of not only its physical transformation, but also of the deeper metamorphosis—the transformation of ideals, of purpose, and of the collective will to reclaim a vision of New Eden that had been lost. As the night deepens and the stars twinkle above, the renewed city seems to breathe in harmony with its people—a harmony that is woven from the threads of hope, unity, and the indomitable spirit that had led them from darkness into the light.

Amidst the joyous season of renewal, when the city's streets are adorned with colorful banners and laughter dances on the air, a summons arrives for Ethan. Dr. Collins requests his presence in his office, a place that had once been shrouded in secrecy but now stands as a space of dialogue and reconciliation.

Ethan enters the office, a sense of curiosity mingling with caution. Dr. Collins stands by the window, his gaze fixed on the night sky, where stars twinkle in a tapestry of mystery.

Dr. Collins: "Ethan, my young friend, there is something I need to share with you—a message we've received from a distant planet."

Ethan's brow furrows, his curiosity piqued. The very idea of a message from beyond their world seems both exhilarating and unnerving.

Dr. Collins taps a holographic screen on his desk, and an ethereal glow fills the room. The message materializes—a series of coded symbols, a language that is both alien and strangely familiar.

Dr. Collins: "This message was received by our satellite arrays. It's encrypted, and the source is a planet we've never encountered before. The message is simple, yet enigmatic—'we are coming.'"

Ethan's gaze narrows, his mind racing to grasp the implications. He turns to Dr. Collins, his voice laced with intrigue.

Ethan: "Who are 'they'? What do they mean by 'we are coming'?"

Dr. Collins' expression holds a mix of intrigue and concern, his eyes reflecting a myriad of thoughts.

Dr. Collins: "That, my young friend, is the question. It could be a greeting, a warning, or something altogether different. And that's where you and Captain Grace Thompson come in."

As if on cue, Captain Grace Thompson enters the room—a presence that exudes strength and resolve. She's been instrumental in decoding messages of all kinds, her military background making her an invaluable asset.

Grace: "Ethan, Dr. Collins is right. This message carries weight, and we need to understand its intent. I've been working on deciphering the code, and I've made some progress."

She motions toward the holographic screen, where the coded symbols shift and rearrange, morphing into comprehensible text.

Grace: "The message decodes to 'we are coming.' But there's more—a second layer hidden within the code."

She presses a button, and the screen changes once more, revealing a hidden message.

Grace: "This layer is a series of coordinates, pinpointing a location—our location."

Ethan's eyes widen, a mixture of awe and apprehension flooding his thoughts.

Ethan: "But why? Why are they coming here?"

Grace's expression remains resolute, but her voice carries a note of urgency that casts a shadow over the room.

Grace: "That's the question, isn't it? And there's something else, something embedded in the coordinates—a sequence that's eerily familiar."

Ethan's heart quickens, a sense of foreboding settling over him.

Ethan: "Familiar? How?"

Grace's gaze meets Ethan's, and her words carry a weight that ripples through the room, sending shivers down spines.

Grace: "Ethan, the sequence—it matches the symbols from the ancient chamber, the same symbols that once spoke of a darker past."

As the weight of her words sinks in, a chill permeates the room. The air seems charged with uncertainty, and as Ethan and Dr. Collins exchange a glance, the realization dawns upon them—a message from the stars, a hidden layer of meaning, and a connection to a past that refuses to be buried.

The season of celebration is suddenly veiled in a cloud of uncertainty—a cloud that carries a question that lingers in the air: Who are they, and what does their arrival truly signify? As laughter and music continue to weave through the streets of the renewed New Eden, a new mystery has taken root—one that hints at a future fraught with unknown challenges and the echoes of history that may yet shape their destinies.

The End.

www.ingramcontent.com/pod-product-compliance
Lightning Source LLC
LaVergne TN
LVHW090940150826
845672LV00006B/1568

* 9 7 9 8 8 9 1 3 3 5 0 6 6 *